Praise for

CAN OF WORMS

"A misfit seventh grader's half-serious conviction that he's an alien proves well-founded in this wild, slime-and-monster-filled romp . . . Fans of such escapades will welcome this with open arms, tentacles, and pseudopods."
—***Kirkus Reviews***

"Told with great humor and imagination . . . sure to be popular with young teens looking for a quick read and lots of laughs."
—***VOYA***

"This humorous, fast-paced science-fiction adventure is set in the real world of adolescent angst, bullies, and first love . . . may just win some new sci-fi fans."
—***School Library Journal***

"Readers who like their sci-fi with a laugh track will enjoy opening this can of worms."
—***The Horn Book***

CAN OF WORMS

KATHY MACKEL

AN AVON CAMELOT BOOK

AVON BOOKS, INC.
1350 Avenue of the Americas
New York, New York 10019

Copyright © 1999 by Kathy Mackel
Published by arrangement with the author
Library of Congress Catalog Card Number: 98-53346
ISBN: 0-380-80050-0
www.avonbooks.com

First Avon Camelot Paperback Printing: March 2000
First Avon Camelot Bookclub Printing: January 2000

CAMELOT TRADEMARK REG. U.S. PAT. OFF. AND IN OTHER COUNTRIES, MARCA REGISTRADA, HECHO EN U.S.A.

Printed in the U.S.A.

OPM 10 9 8 7 6 5 4 3 2 1

To Todd, Sean, and Nicole.

CAN OF WORMS

1

I was only two years old when the Jongs caught up to us.

Imagine a cobra about seven feet tall. Then imagine a humanoid face with mouth, nose, and two eyes. But what eyes—restless, always flicking about. Air holes for a nose, constantly opening and closing, scenting prey. And a round mouth, flexible enough to form speech, but hiding a forked tongue for darting out commands and threats.

If you can imagine that nightmare of a creature, you know the Jongs.

They had two strongly muscled arms that ended in seven-fingered hands on each side of their upper bodies. On their lower bodies, they had many small, jointed legs. As they moved on their many feet, they were swift and silent.

Their heads were hooded, just like the cobras

here on Earth. When the Jongs prepared to attack, their hoods flared and rippled under their body armor. Unlike cobras, however, they weren't poisonous—except for their hateful hearts.

And for whatever insane reason, they spread their venom through the galaxy.

The Jongs had driven us from our homeworld of Hanzel, a shining planet of green trees and crystal skies. Though we left in a hurry, we brought as much of our home with us as we could.

Our spaceship, over a mile long and half that wide, was built for a long journey. The living quarters and work areas were grouped around fields and hills spotted with acres of trees, grass, and glimmering ponds.

I was born on the ship. When I work hard at remembering, I can see scattered pictures, like a flickering video: running through the tall meadow grass, barely able to see over the flower tops. Flying free in the antigravity well. Putting my ear against the long, slick wall to hear and feel the steady vibration that meant we were still moving through space.

I don't remember my parents. But I do remember smiles and hugs and worry on everyone's faces. Although we smaller kids played with no thought of tomorrow, the adults looked ahead to a safe voyage and watched behind for the evil Jongs. Their worry never went away.

I was still very young, maybe no more than two,

when that worry turned to terror and our meadows turned to flame.

Legions of Jongs stormed our ship. They took us by surprise. Maybe they had jumped hyperspace, or had found a wormhole to sneak through. I was playing in the fields when the screaming began. There was panic everywhere. People around me ran for their lives. But our spaceship was a little world and in the end, there was no place to run.

Someone snatched me from the flowering bush where I crouched. My rescuer shoved me under his arm and plunged into a pond. He kicked and paddled toward the bottom while I hung on, terrified. When my air ran out, I swallowed water and then began breathing liquid like a fish. It was cool and smooth in my lungs, and thousands of tiny bubbles trickled out of my mouth.

We pushed into a narrow pipe, tossed hard against the walls by a strong current. My rescuer held me tight until we dumped out into a holding tank. I spit up the water and breathed air again.

We were in a part of the ship I had never seen before—children weren't allowed on the flight deck. I rubbed water from my eyes and never saw my rescuer's face as he shoved me into a pod and strapped me in.

A mist formed over my face and I felt warm and drowsy, safe even though there was chaos all around. Just before I drifted off to sleep, the Jongs stormed into the room. The commander snarled a order and, as the door to my pod shut, I saw laser fire everywhere. There was an explosion and . . .

". . . and then what happened?" Danny yelled.

I sighed. Danny's impatience always wrecked the rhythm of my storytelling.

"I don't know," I said. "That's all I remember."

"Come on, Mike," Danny moaned. "You're not going to tell us how the story ends?" What a whiner. I only put up with him because he idolized me.

I stood up and pulled the foil curtain away from the door of the treehouse. Chills ran up my arms, around my neck, then down my back. Remembering always took a lot out of me. Sunlight sneaked in around the orange and red leaves, and I leaned into its warmth.

"It's not a story," I said. "It's the truth. The confidential truth." I gave my audience a stern look. They knew they were not to repeat the Hanzel Chronicles to anyone. *Anyone.* Who knew if the Jongs had agents here on Earth? Besides, I had enough of a reputation for being weird without my stories of aliens and space battles getting around Ashby Middle School.

"No one outside this circle must know the truth," I repeated.

Nick snickered from the corner of the treehouse. I smacked him in the head with a foam football,

and he shut up. I looked back to the guys si
crosslegged in front of me: Danny Delude, Kur
Perko, and Ben McCoy, all ten-year-olds. And little
Jay Loose, my five-year-old next-door neighbor.
They were my greatest fans, which was the only
reason I allowed them in my treehouse.

"Do you really know how to breathe water?"
Jay asked.

Another rude snort from the corner. Nick
Thorpe was thirteen, a seventh grader like me and
my best friend. I kept him fed, and he kept me
laughing. But sometimes I could just beat the heck
out of him.

Kurt answered for me. "Mike already said,
dumbo. His alien powers are, whaddya call it,
Mike?"

"Dormant."

"Yeah, dormant until his people come back."

"It would be too dangerous for Mike to reveal
himself now," Ben added. "Who knows what the
government would do with him?"

"Stick needles in him!" Jay said with a shiver.

"Cut him open and take out his guts!" Kurt
added.

"Eat his brain," Danny said.

True believers. I had taught them well.

"Okay, everybody out," I said. "Story's over for
the day."

"But, Mike," they chorused.

5

d, and they piled down the ladder,

last and because he was little, I stead-
make sure he'd get over the ladder
n we have another story tomorrow?" he
asked.

I sighed. "I wish they were just stories, Jay."

"You're such a liar," Nick laughed, spraying me with crumbs. As soon as the younger kids had disappeared, we dragged the snacks out of hiding: potato chips, creme cakes, juice drinks.

"You're such an oinker," I said, grabbing the bag of chips away. A gust of October wind dashed through the tree, and the chill grabbed me again, as if more than winter was coming. "Nick?"

"Hmm?"

"The stories do seem so real to me," I told him. "Like I saw them all happening. And sometimes still see them happening."

Nick had grown up with me and the Hanzel Chronicles so he knew better than to laugh. "How could they be real? And how the heck could you be an alien?" he said. "Do you think your parents are in some sort of government conspiracy? Covering up a spaceship crash? Or did they just pick you up off the side of the road one day?"

"Consider this: they don't have any baby pictures of me. Why not?" I asked. "The first one they have is when I went to nursery school. But they have tons of Jill, from the first moment she came home, to her first hot dog, and first Christmas and first steps. She'd burp and they'd take a picture. So why didn't they take my picture when I was first born?"

"Jill probably broke the camera," Nick said with a grin.

"And when I asked them if I could see my birth certificate, they said they couldn't find it."

"So, my parents can't find their car keys half the time," Nick reasoned.

"Yeah, but a birth certificate? That's like the most legal thing you can have."

"So, did you come right out and ask them if you were an alien?" Nick sputtered, slopping down the last crumbs from the chips.

"Yeah," I said. I rubbed my arms. The wind was picking up and I was covered with goosebumps.

"And?"

"They smiled and said, 'Of course not.' Then they hid in Mom's office for three hours and discussed whether or not to send me to a psychologist."

Nick punched my arm. "Well, nuts or not, real or fake, they're good stories. I gotta go do my paper route." He swung over the ladder and disappeared.

Even though I was freezing, I stayed and watched the afternoon deepen into early twilight. It wasn't even suppertime but the sky was the color of deep ocean and filled with mystery. I pushed the branches aside and watched the first star appear. So bright. So far away.

I jumped a mile when Jay stuck his head back into the treehouse. He was so little I didn't hear him sneaking up the ladder. "Hey, Mike?" he said.

"Yeah, what?"

"I was thinking and I just wanted to say something."

"What?" I snapped. A cloud moved in the sky and hid my star.

"I'm sorry you got lost from your people," Jay whispered, then he climbed back down through the leaves. He scampered through my backyard, pushed open the gate to his yard, and disappeared.

I was sorry, too.

2

"GO GET 'EM, BUCK," MY DAD YELLED IN FRONT OF a thousand people, including all of my schoolmates at Ashby Middle School.

He made me nuts when he called me Buck. My name is Albert Michael Pillsbury, and I prefer to be called Mike. My dad called me Buck because, he said, "a hardy nickname will add strength to your character, Buck."

My mom called me Alberto because she wanted me to be fluent in Spanish before I turned fourteen. Then on to French, Russian, and German. I wonder how you say Albert in Chinese? With my luck, it's Buck.

My classmates called me weird, and that's when they were being nice. Just because I was somewhat of a genius, it didn't mean I deserved to be called geek, nerd, doofball, or whatever the latest slang for smart kid was.

I tried my best not to be weird. I wore contact lenses instead of my thick glasses. Even though it killed me, I let my sister Jill pick out clothes for me so I wouldn't be caught wearing high-water pants and white socks. I kept my mouth shut in class so no one realized I knew the answer before the teacher even asked the question.

But as hard as I tried, I couldn't quite seem to click with seventh-grade society. And every time my chest ached because I was desperate to be in the middle of things, I looked to the stars and thought it was okay that I didn't fit in. Because I wasn't really supposed to be here anyway.

"Play hard, Buck." My father's cheers rose above the heavy hum of the crowd. I stole a look at my teammates to see if anyone heard the Buck stuff. They were into their pre-game warm-up and the growling, grunting, and screaming that would fire up the desire to kill, kill, kill.

I would just be happy not to be killed, killed, killed.

We were halfway through the season. So far I had escaped injury, mostly because I hadn't been off the bench yet. I had signed up for football in a moment of weakness. My father had been all over me about developing character and toughness so I joined the football team, thinking it would get him off my case.

Bad logic. Dad couldn't be happier. He wasn't

deterred by the fact that I never played. "Give it time, Buck," he said. "It's a new challenge."

My football career had become a family affair. That night, like every Friday night, my family claimed the front row of the bleachers at the 50-yard line. My dad, Dana Pillsbury, wore a big grin and his bright red Ashby Middle School booster jacket. My mom, Pamela Pillsbury, wore a cashmere coat over her black business suit. She nestled her electronic organizer in her gloved hands, glancing at it when she thought I wasn't looking.

My sixteen-year-old sister Jill, there only because my parents insisted, sat next to Mom. She looked like she was sucking on a pickle. "If you sign up for basketball, I'll murder you," she snarled to me after my second game.

No way. I wasn't going to sign up for anything ever again—at least until NASA announced the first manned mission to Mars or Jupiter.

If I wasn't killed, killed, killed first.

By the second quarter Ashby was clobbering Pepperell, 34 to zip. Coach Tremblay's eyes roamed the bench. Don't put me in, I prayed. "Stewart, Vogel, Crupi, front line," he growled. I let out a sigh of relief. Then, "Pillsbury, go to safety."

I pulled on my helmet and trudged out to midfield. We were on defense after Ashby had scored yet another touchdown. The ref stood with his hands on his hips, waiting for the subs to find our places. I stood to the far left of the line.

"Pillsbury!" Scott Schreiber glowered at me from midfield. "Where the heck are you supposed to be?"

"Safety," I said, thinking safety was a relative term in this game.

"Over there, you jerk." Even though he was a seventh grader and first year player like me, Scott was the captain of the team. He was big, strong, and talented. Girls thought he was good-looking.

"Move it," he hollered. The Pepperell center snapped the ball and the quarterback backpedaled, winding up for a pass. I found a running back and tried to stick with him. He darted back and forth, up and down, in and out. I was getting dizzy when, out of nowhere, something hit me in the stomach. I grabbed hard and found a leather missile in my hands.

The football.

In the stands, Dad was hysterical. "Interception! Run, Buck! Run!"

"Run!" my teammates yelled.

"Get him," the Pepperell guys screamed.

The goalposts rose like twin beacons out of the night haze.

I ran for dear life, ignoring the shouts and the feet pounding after me. The diagonal lines of the end zone came into focus and I gripped the football to my chest, trying to disregard all those hulking

Pepperell kids stomping after me, charging to take me down. I could see the white lines, sharp now. Clear. Bright. The end zone was only a few feet away. And then . . .

Something hit me. Hard. I hit the ground, even harder.

But the darkness that hit me was the hardest of all.

Lights burst through the haze, blinding me. I was wet and chilled to the bone, and as the bulky figure leaned over me, fear gripped me.

The creature wore battle gear and a helmet. Even though I could barely see, I knew it was a Jong. The beast garbled some words at me, but its speech was slurred by its forked tongue. I understood one phrase: "the brain."

And then I knew. I knew why they had persecuted my people, chased us across the galaxy.

"They want my brain," I mumbled.

The Jong reached for my face.

"No!" I screamed as I struggled to rise. "NO!"

"Calm down," another Jong said.

"They want to eat my brain!" I screamed as I thrashed on the ground, trying to get up.

All the Jongs started laughing.

"He's all right," one of them said.

"Just as weird as ever," the biggest one said and bent back down. His eyes were snaky and his breath

was hot, reeking of bubblegum. He clawed at the strap of his helmet and tugged it off.

He was going to eat my brain right there. I started screaming again, "No, NO! Leave my brain alone!"

The Jong's helmet came off and . . .

. . . Scott Schreiber sneered at me. "You are a first degree headcase, Pillsbury," he said.

Coach Tremblay and the team trainer pushed through my teammates. "You all right?"

I sat up and saw the October night and the bright field lights.

"What happened?" I asked as the trainer helped me to my feet.

"You took a hard hit," Coach said. "You sure you're okay?"

"I'm fine," I said as I headed for the bench. Coach nodded at the ref, who blew the halftime whistle. "Did I score?" I asked.

Coach Tremblay snorted. "No son, you didn't score." Then he shook his head and walked away.

Scott grabbed my arm. "Wanna know why you didn't score, smart boy?"

"Uh, why?" I asked.

"Because I tackled you, that's why."

"You?" I thought my head had cleared. Maybe not. "*You* tackled me?"

"That's right, genius. I tackled you."

"How come?" I asked.

"Because you were heading for the wrong goal, you Fruit Loop. If I hadn't stopped you, you would have scored a safety for Pepperell."

For the first time in my life, I felt truly stupid. Scott sensed that—his grin lit up like a firecracker.

"I—I must have gotten turned around wrong," I stammered.

"Sure, Pillsbury. Maybe you were confused. It happens." He play-punched my shoulder and smiled. "But maybe . . ."

"Maybe what?"

"Maybe someone ate your brain," he whispered. Then he shoved me and dashed to the locker room, howling with laughter the whole way.

3

THERE was statistically a very slim chance that I was an alien. How incredible to have crash-landed on Earth as a baby, been rescued by Earthlings and raised as their own, and not have anyone say a word about it. Couldn't happen, right? Except, in my darkest moments, I knew that if something as incredible as that did happen, everyone would keep it a secret. Even from me.

I knew a lot of adopted kids. Willie Clark came from Korea, and Mei-Ling Abramson came from China. Tommy Kerasi was adopted when he was one year old, after being in foster care. Mandy Bachmann came to her new family as an infant. All the adopted kids I knew had been told they were adopted, and were happy to be where they were.

My parents refused to admit I was adopted.

When I was seven or eight, I had demanded to see my birth certificate. They said they lost it when we moved, and they'd get a new one to show me— sometime. But that sometime never came.

Same thing with the baby pictures, lost in the move. Mom even cried a little. "You were such a beautiful baby." But how would I know when we didn't have any baby pictures of me?

I certainly didn't resemble anyone in my family. My dad was short and very strong. He was a star hockey forward and baseball catcher. He was bright, too. He went to Dartmouth and then Wharton Business School. When I hit junior high school, I grew taller by the moment and was built like a string bean. I tried every sport there was and never learned to hit a baseball or kick a soccer ball or skate with ease.

My dad loved to win. Not that he would ever cheat or anything. But everything in his life was a competition and he gave it his all. That's why he loved his job. He was a stockbroker—a very competitive profession—and he could tell moment by moment whether he was succeeding or failing.

I never cared about winning or losing.

My mom was small. She was also very beautiful, with auburn hair and bright blue eyes. Mom small, dad small, me tall. Didn't fit, did it? Also, my dad had hazel eyes and light brown hair. My dark brown hair and green eyes were a genetic possibility but very unlikely.

Mom was very cultured and personable. As the director of international marketing for a pharmaceutical company, she knew how to make anyone feel instantly at ease, whether it was the president of a huge company or the guy who came to fix our septic tank.

I could barely string two sentences together—unless I was telling the Hanzel Chronicles. Then the words flowed like a river, with a power of their own.

My sister, Jill, had my mom's hair and my dad's eyes. The guys in the high school, most of whom were obviously morons, thought she was gorgeous. She had a zillion friends. She played field hockey and softball and, just like she had to go to my games, I had to go to hers.

She hated me. That was the only reason I thought I might be a real part of this family.

My parents did their best to make me feel loved. They even worked at home a lot so they would be around for Jill and me. But I just didn't feel a connection. I didn't understand why making money grow made my dad so happy, and why dealing with difficult people made my mom happy. They never understood why I would rather hang out in my treehouse and tell amazing stories than join sports teams and drama groups and science clubs.

They claimed to view the Hanzels as a childish fixation that I would outgrow. Either they were covering up a conspiracy or they just didn't understand me.

I thought the Hanzels were an amazing truth still waiting to be discovered.

That Friday night, I tossed and turned until about midnight. Jong commandos tackled me as the goalposts burst into flame. I knew I wouldn't get any sleep until I told my parents that I had decided to quit football.

I crept downstairs, my knees and back still sore from Scott's hard hit. I went into the downstairs wing—the big addition off our kitchen where my parents had their home offices. Some moms and dads watch late-night TV; my parents went back to work after my sister and I went to bed.

I stood outside my mother's office, watching her through the French doors. Even in her soft green jogging suit, Mom looked like the skilled executive. She wore a headset and spoke rapidly in Russian. She motioned me in and continued the conversation. When it was her turn to listen, she slipped her fingers over the mouthpiece of her headset and whispered, "A nervous client. I won't be much longer." Then she was off to the Russian races again.

I wandered around her office. She had a large,

glass-topped desk and a deep maroon leather chair. She didn't sit; she seemed more comfortable pacing. The rug was a wine color and the walls were cream, filled with prints of wildflowers. There was a comfortable sofa and two chairs and a side table with family photos. My mother seemed more at home here than anywhere in the house.

She spoke her Russian farewells and clicked off the handset. *"¿Como estas, Alberto? ¿Estas infermo?"*

"No, I'm fine," I said.

She caught the irritation in my voice and dropped the Spanish.

"Can't sleep?"

"No," I said, trying to figure out how to break the news that I was quitting football. Pillsburys never quit anything.

Mom waited patiently. She's big on giving her children what she calls "space." I tried to think of the most diplomatic way to phrase this. I didn't think she would take kindly to me confessing, "I stink therefore I quit."

Her phone buzzed. She looked quickly at it then smiled back at me.

"Aren't you going to answer that?" I asked.

"It can wait. What's on your mind, Mike?"

Buzz, buzz, buzz. "You can answer that," I said.

"Later," she said. "Everything okay?" Buzz,

buzz. Mom folded one hand over the other and cracked her knuckles.

"Everything's fine, Mom," I said and kissed her cheek.

It wasn't until I pulled the door closed behind me that my mother picked up her phone. She smiled at me through the glass windows of the French doors and mouthed, "I love you."

And she was off to the races again, this time in Chinese.

Dad's office was hung with photos of sports legends, many autographed. My favorite was the poster of my father, wearing Dartmouth green and slapping a puck past a stunned goalie in Harvard crimson.

Dad's furniture was dark leather, creased and worn. His oak floor was littered with scraps of paper. Dad never just threw paper away; he had to cram it into a ball and toss it at the trash. The center of his office held a huge oak table with four computers. Each one was strung with a dozen cables, heavily networked to the world's financial centers. My father was so fanatical about monitoring the markets that we had a gas generator in our backyard in case we lost power.

Dad never lost power. Even though it was late at night, my dad was still crackling with energy. Like Mom, he also wore a headset. But he wasn't

21

pacing; he fidgeted in his chair, eyes glued to his multiple monitors. As he shouted into the phone, he pounded his desk for emphasis. "The Nikkei's all over the place. Wacko." He nodded a hello to me. "Get fifty K of the Oshai. We'll escrow the rest until London opens."

Dad clicked off his phone but kept his eyes on the monitors. "You okay, Buck?"

"I'm fine," I said. I looked at John Elway's photo hanging over Dad's head. One of the greatest quarterbacks of all time. My dad loved football. If I couldn't break the news to my mother, how could I ever tell my father?

Dad looked away from the screen as if he were reading my mind. "Tough break tonight." Then he whipped his head back, read a line of numbers, and slapped his hand on his desk. "All right! I called that one, right on the money!" He reached for the handset to his phone, looking back to me as he dialed. "Just hang in there, kid."

I took a deep breath, trying to breathe in some guts. "What if I—"

Dad snapped back to the screen. "Oh no," he cried, then finished his dialing. "What do we have in the Zurich account?" he yelled.

"—don't want to?" I finished in a soft voice.

Dad kept his eyes on the monitor as he yelled his instructions. "Okay. Move half into—I don't

22

care. Don't wuss out on me now. You wanna play with the big boys, you gotta—"

Then he paused, and though he was talking into his phone, he looked straight at me. "—play to win," he said with deliberate emphasis. "You gotta play to win."

Then he came over and gave me the biggest hug in the world, as if he could squeeze his power into me.

4

I KNEW I WAS IN TROUBLE WHEN SCOTT CAME into computer class, surrounded by his buddies. I'm not much of a fighter, but I'm not particularly afraid of bullies like Scott and Ryan and Terry.

It was Drew who worried me.

Drew Mikalski is the second smartest kid in the seventh grade. I'm the first and for years we were inseparable. But he got into test scores and class standings and academic awards, and I got bored with competing.

When I saw Scott whispering to Drew, I poked Nick. "Schreiber's up to something."

Nick glanced up from his game of solitaire. "You want me to beat him up now or later?" he wisecracked.

Scott strutted over to us. "So, Pillsbury," he drawled.

"So, Schreiber," I drawled back.

"How's your brain?" he asked.

"At least Mike has one." Nick snickered. His mouth always works faster than his brain. Scott grabbed Nick's ears and levitated him.

Nick was turning purple just as Mrs. Nickerson came in. "In your seats, class." I zoned out Mrs. Nickerson's lesson. This was the second week in October but I had already finished the year's work. She knew it and allowed me to work independently as long as I didn't disturb the class. I was deep into writing my latest Chronicle when Katelyn Sands came in.

She was the one person worth staying on Earth for.

Katelyn had long, light brown hair. When she tossed her head, her hair moved like silk. Her eyes were dark brown and she had short, curly lashes. She was quick to smile and quicker to laugh.

Katelyn was nice to everyone, even Jimmy Dugan who didn't shower and Judy Cryan who was mean to everyone. I thought if I could have Katelyn as my friend—or in my wildest dreams, my girlfriend—I would never have to worry about winning or losing or making a good impression or saying the right thing.

Katelyn was the kind of girl you could just be yourself with. Except I liked her so much that I turned into a stone dummy when she was around.

Because she was late for class, she had to take the only seat that was left. "Hi Mike," she said in a low voice. "Okay if I sit here?"

Mind? I would move mountains just to sit next to Katelyn. "I suppose." Some genius. Nick kicked me and I kicked him back.

"You all know what to do. Get started," Mrs. Nickerson said.

The class was studying word processing, something I had been doing since second grade. I concentrated on the Hanzels until Drew and Scott turned in their seats and smirked at me. What were they up to?

Mrs. Nickerson reached for her mug. She always grabbed a cup of coffee during our class. As soon as the door swooshed closed behind her, Scott poked Ryan and Terry. Drew raised his right hand with a flourish and hit the ENTER key on his keyboard.

Seconds later my screen flashed: *you have mail.* I ignored it. Drew sent me more mail, this time with an audible alarm. *Beep beep beep.* Heads turned and I had no choice but to double-click on my mail.

The message was in bold letters: **I HAVE YOUR BRAIN**.

I clicked it off. The next message arrived. **BUT I'LL GIVE IT BACK**.

I clicked it off and waited, holding my breath.

All the screens in the class flickered. Katelyn jerked back in surprise. I did a quick calculation, wondering if I could crash the network before Drew did his damage. But I was too late. All the screens lit up with: **MIKE PILLSBURY HAS MUSH FOR BRAINS**.

And underneath, in its full digital glory, was a steaming pile of cow manure.

The class exploded with hoots and howls. Mr. Martin stomped in from next door and threatened to call Mrs. Nickerson. The class shut up but, after Mr. Martin left I was assaulted with silent laughter, pointing fingers, and nasty faces. Only Katelyn got back to work.

I checked the wall clock—about four minutes before Mrs. Nickerson would return from coffee. Time enough for revenge.

I hacked into the school's network. By the second week in September I had decoded all the passwords. We had just had yearbook pictures taken and they were stored digitally on the file server in the office. After a couple of clicks, I had the picture I wanted. I reached into my backpack and pulled out the box of diskettes that I carry around for emergencies.

With about sixty seconds to spare, I was ready. I hit the ENTER key and for the second time that morning, all the monitors flickered. Everyone turned to Drew, who shrugged a *not me*. Scott shifted in his seat. A quick line of sweat formed on his forehead.

Every monitor filled with glorious orange and red flames. And then, the screens cleared and the class got mooned by the back end of a half-ton hog. There's nothing more disgusting than fat, slimy, pig butt wiggling in your face. The hog dropped in the muck and rolled onto its back, its pointy hooves dancing in the air.

My sound effects started: snorting, grunting, bellowing, and then the ultimate—the half-ton ham passed a thousand cubic liters of barnyard gas.

My classmates roared with laughter as the hog righted itself and shook its blubbery belly, flinging globs of mud and garbage. The porker wagged its twiggly tail and then began to turn in slow motion toward the camera. Its hulking front shoulders came into range, then its pointy ears, then its broad snout in profile. As it turned full face, the class let out a collective gasp.

The pig wore Scott Schreiber's face.

Touchdown.

5

THE RAIN POURED OUTSIDE, COLD AND ANGRY. I huddled in my bedroom, Nick and the squirts clustered around me, ready for a new chapter in the Hanzel Chronicles.

Now the Jongs weren't the only enemies of my people. The first war was fought with the Mantix. . . .

"Howdya know all this, Mike?" Danny chimed in.

"I told you, it's in my genes."

"What jeans?" Jay asked. "Those jeans?" he said, poking at my pants.

"Shut up," Ben growled. I waved him quiet. Jay deserved an answer.

"The information is stored inside me. Locked inside my brain," I explained. "To prepare me for when my people come back for me." I took a long, dramatic pause, dropping my head a bit. "If any of them survived."

Nick snickered from his position of privilege—my top bunk. Someday . . .

As cruel and wicked as the Jongs were, they were not without friends. The Mantix, who resembled overgrown sewer rats, were their allies. Whenever the Jongs needed dirty work done, the Mantix were more than happy to do it.

Years before I was born, Hanzel was a planet of peace and prosperity. My people were successful merchants throughout our corner of the galaxy, known for honesty and craftsmanship. There was no pollution or crime, and we lived in harmony among green trees and clear waters.

It was a day like any day here on Earth. Adults were busy in the farms, factories, and business centers. Kids were in school, learning how to read and write and fly.

"Whaddya mean fly? Like in planes?" Ben asked.

"Spaceships," Kurt said.

"Body rockets," Danny chimed in.

"Nothing!" I snapped. "We didn't need anything to make us fly. We just flew."

Jay flapped his little arms, and I was about to correct him but I thought, what the heck. Let him figure out his own reality.

We all flew. Babies learning to walk would natu-

rally float a few inches from the ground, then settle back. Developing the skill to rise into the air and navigate took patience and years of training.

But our abilities to breathe underwater and to fly in the air couldn't save us that day.

It started in the town square. Hanzel had such beautiful weather that most stores sold their merchandise in open-air bazaars. Men and women strolled through the streets, the two suns shining overhead, the sky a pale blue, the air sweet and warm. No one noticed as the roots of the trees began to buckle.

In the park, parents watched their toddlers as they ran and jumped and fluttered. No one noticed as the crystal green pond rippled outward from the center.

In the schoolyard, kids played a game similar to baseball, stationing fielders twenty feet in the air to catch high flies. No one noticed as the infield started to erupt in puffs of dust.

A day like any other. No one noticed anything was wrong.

Until we were overrun.

On orders from the Jongs, the Mantix invaded. Not from the sky but from the ground under our feet. Hordes of Mantix broke through the streets, the fields, the play yards. Even the oceans swarmed with them.

The intruders were unarmed except for the nasty

mucous glands in their pointed snouts. No shooting or stabbing—instead they slimed us into submission. Not like that gross stuff you buy in the toy store or that green stuff in the movies. This was diabolic ooze that hardened on contact.

Imagine this: you're going about your business when the ground erupts around you. An army of five-foot long rats crawls from underfoot and scurries everywhere. Once you recover from shock, you rise into the air, trying to escape. But the Mantix spit on you and you're doused in foul-smelling goo. As you go to wipe it from your face, you realize it's hardening. Within seconds you can't move. You can't help yourself—you begin to scream. But your scream echoes back at you, trapped within the frozen Mantix slime. You scream and scream and . . .

Jay screamed, his cries rattling the windows. Startled, Nick toppled off the top bunk. "Jeepers, Pillsbury, your stories are getting too good," he laughed.

Jay pointed behind me, and I realized it wasn't the Chronicles that had frightened him. It was my sister Jill, wearing four-inch curlers on her head and a green mudpack on her face.

"Shut that kid up," she said. Danny grabbed Jay and shushed him.

"Get lost," I said.

"Fine," Jill said. "I didn't want to tell you about your guest anyway."

"What guest?" I asked.

"Sorry. I've been told to get lost," she sneered and turned to leave.

"Wait. I'm—I'm sorry."

"Sorry what?"

"I am sorry, most exalted sister."

Jill studied her fingernails. They alternated gold and silver. "Katelyn what's-her-name wants to see you."

"Katelyn?" I said, awestruck. "Katelyn Sands?"

"Whatever." Jill stepped out into the hall. "Hey, you can come on up," she yelled.

Up? To my room? With my space toys and stupid fifth-grade friends in plain view? I hauled Danny and Kurt to their feet and shoved them at the door. "Out! Everyone out!"

"How come?" Jay looked like he was about to cry.

"Because Mike's *girlfriend* is here," Nick said.

"You got a girlfriend?" Ben asked.

"No," I said as I opened the door. Light footsteps pranced up the stairs. I yanked Kurt back and slammed the door.

"I thought you wanted us out," Kurt said.

Katelyn couldn't see all these little kids. She would think I was a social misfit. Sure, I had some seventh-grade friends but none of them—except for Nick—had any imagination.

"In my closet," I whispered. Confused but used

to obeying my orders, the guys piled in. "Not a sound," I warned. Kurt giggled. "Or I'll tell the Mantix," I added. Kurt shut up and Jay grabbed Ben's arm.

I kicked the toy rockets and action figures under my bed. Then I realized I didn't know where Nick had gone. Mr. Big Mouth. Ready to snicker on a moment's notice.

"Mike?" Katelyn called through the door.

My heart almost stopped. I took a deep breath and let her in.

"Hey," she said with a smile. "How's it going?"

Like I was about to have a heart attack, that's how. "Uh, okay," I mumbled.

Katelyn looked around. "Cool," she said.

"Uh, cool?" Some genius, with my two-word vocabulary.

"The space and alien stuff. You're really into it." My walls were filled with posters of colorful planets, exploding suns, and racy spaceships.

"Yeah, I guess." I knew I should make small talk, but my mouth felt like a Mantix had slimed it shut.

"I want to ask a favor," Katelyn said.

Snicker. There he was, hiding under my desk. I waved my foot in Nick's face as a warning.

"What was that?" Katelyn asked.

I forced the words out. "Uh . . . my computer. I programmed it to make all sorts of sounds."

Nick snickered again. I kicked him. Best friend or not, someday . . .

"That's why I'm here! I know how good you are with computers and all."

I had taught Scott a lesson. So why did I feel so embarrassed about my pig masterpiece?

"Scott is a jerk," Katelyn said, as if she had read my mind.

"Yeah," I said.

"Anyway, Mike, the reason I'm here . . ." She paused and I wondered exactly why she was there. What could the most popular girl in seventh grade want with weird Mike Pillsbury? "I'm the chairperson of the Halloween dance, and I want to show the eighth graders how cool we can be. You know, put on a dance like they've never dreamed of. So I need decorating help."

"You mean, like hanging streamers and stuff?"

Katelyn grinned. "Let me tell you what I had in mind." Even Nick stopped snickering as Katelyn outlined her plans. She was much more than just a pretty face. Her ideas were brilliant.

Maybe life on Earth wasn't so boring after all.

6

THE NEXT TWO WEEKS WERE THE HAPPIEST OF MY life. I stuck with football because I didn't have the nerve to tell the flawless Dana and Pamela Pillsbury that their chicken son wanted to quit. But more importantly, Katelyn played field hockey and I got to see her every afternoon at the field. Every day after practice, we met in the computer lab.

Katelyn planned a multimedia show for the dance. Mrs. Nickerson let me use her powerhouse PC to digitize old videos of *Frankenstein, Dracula, Werewolf,* and other horror classics. I mixed golden oldies with rock music, integrating the sounds and images with a light show. We planned to use my laptop and Principal Goodrich's screen projector to display the show on a wall that was forty feet long and eighteen feet high.

The best part was the opening song, a rock tune

the radio had been playing for two weeks now: "Ghoul's Night Out."

Listen to the werewolf howl
Beware, you'll see the monster scowl
The vampire grins a toothy smile
The zombie spins in deadpan style

Watch out! They're out!
They're coming out to play.
So don't get in their way
It's Ghoul's night out.

Katelyn and I laughed as we thought of kids coming into the cafeteria, seeing the same old pumpkin and goblin decorations, then being blasted with dancing monsters, flashing lights, and booming music. A truly ghoulish get-together. With Katelyn's creativity and my computer skills, we knew we would pull it off to perfection.

Our first two days working together, Katelyn talked and I grunted.

"Mrs. Nickerson was really nice to let us use all the equipment," Katelyn would say.

"Yep," I would say and feverishly type more commands.

"Science class was great today," Katelyn would say. "I never knew that cows had four stomachs. Did you?"

"Nope," I would say and double-click my mouse.

By Wednesday, I forgot how she could never be interested in someone as weird as me, and we had a real conversation. "What's your family like?" she asked.

"I have two perfect parents and a stuck-up sister. Jill's nose is so far up in the air, it could be a weather satellite."

Katelyn laughed, then her eyes darkened. "Must be nice to have perfect parents," she said with a faraway look.

"Are you kidding?" I yelped. "They never do anything stupid or unfashionable or even mean. Try living up to those role models!"

"Better than my family," she said. "My mother works at the hospital all day and soaks her sore feet all night. And my dad is either watching a baseball game, reading a baseball magazine, or computing the latest baseball statistics. My little sister—she's always crying about something. And speaking of noses, her nose is always running and she wipes it on her sleeve."

"Gross," I said, then laughed when I imagined Jill's nose stuck in the air and starting to run. It was feel-good-in-the-stomach laughter, the kind I had with Nick and the guys.

On Friday Katelyn asked me what it was like being the smartest kid in seventh grade.

"Rotten," I mumbled. "Everyone thinks I'm weird."

"How could it be rotten?" she cried. "You always have the answers. You never have to sweat any tests or homework."

"Let me give you an example," I explained. "I tried playing Little League. My teammates were just trying to keep track of balls and strikes. But I had to measure the distance to the pitchers mound and time the pitch and do the calculations for how fast the pitcher was throwing. They all thought I was weird but I *had* to know. I don't know why, I just *had* to."

"Seems reasonable to me," Katelyn said. "Any information helps you do better."

"Yeah," I said, relieved that she understood. "What about you?" I asked. "Do you ever feel—?"

"Weird?" she said, then laughed when I nodded. "No, not weird. That's not the right word. More like obligated."

"Obligated?" I asked.

"Yeah, like I have to please everyone. Not so they'll like me—I know that wouldn't be right. But to get everyone to work together. To keep my mom and dad from fighting when her feet hurt and he wants my sister quiet so he can watch TV. To keep the kids at school from being jerks and get them to be nice to each other. I don't like it when people don't get along."

"Me neither," I said. "But sometimes I think I'm so weird I'll never get along."

"Mike. You do get along. Stop worrying about it," Katelyn said.

"Okay," I said. "I'll stop worrying if you'll stop worrying."

We both laughed. "A deal," Katelyn said, and I believed her.

By Monday of the next week we could phone each other, and "Hi" was enough to let us know who was calling. We finished each other's sentences and we laughed most of the time. We sat together in computer and science class.

On Tuesday, in front of the whole seventh grade, Katelyn ate lunch with Nick and me. Her friends gave her surprised looks but grabbed their trays and followed her to our table. Nick was silent, probably for the first time in his life. He was in the presence of a miracle and we both knew it.

I just didn't know how long it could last.

7

"PILLSBURY, ONTO THE FRONT LINE. NOSE GUARD,"
Coach Tremblay barked.

"But I never play nose guard," I stammered.

"You do today," he shouted.

I scooted forward and planted myself in the three-point stance. Across from me was Ryan at center; behind him, Scott Schreiber was ready for the snap.

"Take him down," Tremblay growled in my ear as he prowled behind the defense.

"Huh?" I asked.

"Sack him!"

"But this is practice, Coach."

"If we don't give Schreiber strong medicine in practice, what's he gonna do if someone pounds him out during a game?" The coach had a point, but I didn't think I was the one to be teaching Scott Schreiber a lesson. Especially about football.

"Hut one, hut two, hut three," Scott yelled. The center snapped the ball and we charged forward. My assignment: get to Scott before he passed the ball.

Impossible. And yet, as the offensive line shifted to protect their quarterback, a small opening appeared. I darted through and skipped sideways as a blocker leaped for me. He tumbled at my feet and there was only green grass separating me from Scott.

Pass the ball, I prayed, knowing I couldn't touch him once his hands were empty. But he danced back, looking down field and not aware of me bearing down on him. I lowered my head and rammed him in the chest. He staggered but didn't fall. His eyes flashed with surprise through the bars of his helmet. He swiped at me with his left hand while he nestled the ball in his right arm and lunged forward.

I grabbed his knees and hung on with all my might. After a few seconds of struggling forward, Scott toppled face first. *Oomph.*

Coach Tremblay whistled the play dead. "Schreiber," he roared. "Is that ball glued to your hands? You had two open receivers! You trying to decide which girl you like best?"

"Coach, it's just that . . ." Scott stammered, looking for an explanation.

". . . it's just that Pillsbury rang your chimes,"

the coach snapped. Even Ryan and Terry joined the laughter. "Okay, everyone to the showers," Coach ordered. "Nice job, Pillsbury."

I piled equipment in my arms and was heading for the storage shed when I was shoved from behind. The orange marker cones tumbled onto the grass. "What the—?"

"Nice job, Pillsbury," Scott sing-songed his voice, mocking Coach's words.

"Still picking grass out of your faceguard?" I said, gathering up the cones.

"You're gonna be picking my foot out of your butt," Scott growled.

"You wish," I said. I opened the shed and stacked the cones inside.

"I mean it, Pillsbury, you're ticking me off."

My hands started to shake so I clenched them in fists and knocked them together. "And you're boring me, Schreiber," I said with as much courage as I could muster without throwing up. Maybe I was afraid of bullies after all.

"I'm gonna get you, Pillsbury," he snarled. "You are gonna be so sorry."

I took a deep breath and willed my feet not to run. "I already am. Sorry that you're such a loser." I walked away, feeling his eyes burning through my back.

The sky was a deep blue and the stars were coming out when I pushed through the gate into

43

my backyard. It was a warm night, maybe the last one left before Halloween. The smell of beef stew coming from the kitchen window made my stomach rumble. The knots from the encounter with Scott were unwinding, and I was starved.

The leaves in the big elm rustled. My treehouse was decked with its foil shell, converting it to a space ship. A tiny light flickered through the cracks.

Nick and the squirts yelped when I stuck my head in. "What's going on in here?" I demanded. The treehouse was my domain and no one, not even Nick, was allowed in without an invitation.

"Nick's telling us about the Lobotomies," Danny said.

"The Lobotomies?" I glared at Nick. He shrugged.

"Noses like elephants," Danny chimed.

Ben disagreed. "Those are trunks, dummy."

"Not on a Lobotomy, dummy. Ask Nick. They have long noses that shoot acid. Boiling hot acid."

Kurt put in his two cents. "Scariest snot in the universe!"

Even Jay was entranced. "The lobo . . . lobots . . . the whatevers are more dangerous than the Jongs and the Mantix."

"Everyone out now!" I yelled.

"But we're just getting started," Danny whined.

"NOW!" They jumped for the ladder. I grabbed

the back of Nick's shirt and held him until the younger boys disappeared.

"What do you think you're doing?" I asked.

"What you're too busy to do," Nick said. "Keeping the Chronicles going."

"You have no right to do that."

"Like you own the stories?"

"They're about me, aren't they?"

"And you're too good for us. Right?" Nick's voice was edgy.

"What do you mean by that?"

"You spend all your time either pretending to play football or hanging out with the dance committee. You don't need us anymore."

"That's not true. I'm just busy right now. With Katelyn and all that," I stuttered.

"Don't fool yourself, Mike. You're too weird for a girl like Katelyn. She's gonna use you and lose you." Nick hopped over the side and disappeared down the ladder. But his words stayed with me.

"Like you did to us."

After supper, I was carrying out the trash when I heard a crunch in the leaves. "What are you doing here?" I asked Jay.

"I left my glasses in the treehouse," he said, backing against the fence as if I might yell again.

I took his hand. "Come on, we'll go get them." I steadied him up the ladder. A warm wind blew hazy clouds across the bright stars. I sat down and let my legs dangle.

"When I was in kindergarten, I was in bed by this time," I said.

"I always sneak out after my bedtime," Jay said.

"How come?"

"In case the Hanzels come for you. I don't want to miss them."

"Oh." Jay was my truest believer. I patted the floor and Jay sat down. We stared at the constellations. "There's the Big Dipper," I said. "It points to Polaris, the North Star. Sailors used to sight on the star to navigate their ships."

"Nick says you're too busy to tell the Chronicles."

"Everyone knows that Nick is nuts."

"Nick just makes them up. I like the stories when you tell them because then I know they're real." He gazed off into the night sky.

"Yeah, they are real," I said, falling under the spell of the warm wind and the crystal stars. Were the Hanzels real and Katelyn just a dream? Or was Katelyn real and the Hanzels a childish, weird pastime? This October night seemed magic, and anything seemed possible.

"Tell me one now," Jay said. "A Chronicle no one else knows."

"Did I ever tell you how much my people love to dance?" I asked. Jay shook his head.

When I am reunited with my people, we will have a glorious celebration. We'll build a Hanzel ballroom where the floors are so shiny that the light of the stars and moons reflect from above and below. I'll wear a tuxedo with a tie the color of the Hanzel ocean. I'll bow to the loveliest maiden at the ball— a shining lady with light brown hair flowing down her slender back. She'll be dressed in a gown woven from silk and moonlight, and the gems around her neck will glow like stars. I will take her hand. She'll come into my arms and fit just right.

Did I ever tell you that the Hanzels can hear the music of the universe? We'll pause, listening for the music that binds the heavens in perfect harmony. When it sings in our hearts, we'll move to it, swirling like stardust in the solar wind. Our feet will leave the floor and we'll rise into the sky.

And all our dreams will come true.

8

THE air bristled as if electricity sparked from kid to kid to kid. For the seventh graders, it was our first formal dance. The girls stood and giggled, glancing at the boys who tried to hang cool but tugged at their collars and smoothed their hair. The eighth graders pretended to be bored but they shuffled and twisted their feet in anticipation.

As I stood waiting for Mrs. Nickerson to unlock the cafeteria, my stomach turned and rolled. I had it all planned: I would ask Katelyn to dance and then, as long as I didn't step on her feet or do something equally as stupid, I would ask her to go out with me. Then I saw her, pushing through the crowd to get to me, and my heart stopped. She wore a blue pullover sweater the color of the warm summer sky. Her short dark skirt flowed with every step she took. Her long hair hung loose on her shoulders and her smile was brighter than ever.

"Sorry I'm late," she whispered. I could smell rose blossoms and spearmint gum.

"Is the dance committee finally ready?" Mrs. Nickerson asked. Her voice was stern but she winked at me as if she could read my mind.

Katelyn nodded and Mrs. Nickerson unlocked the cafeteria. We slipped in ahead of the crowd. Katelyn ran to each table to light the battery-driven candles in the pumpkin centerpieces. Kids streamed in behind her. I reached for the power switch that would light the main display—a string of orange lights in the shape of a giant skull. Katelyn and I decided to wait until all the kids were inside before we lit it.

We wanted to hear the *oohs* and *aahs*.

When the cafeteria was mobbed, I hit the dimmer switch. The noise settled with the darkness. Then I hit the power. BAM! Bright orange filled the far wall. As we expected, the kids gasped in wonder.

Then laughed.

Mrs. Nickerson chuckled. "Michael Pillsbury, how adorable."

Adorable? The lights were supposed to form a frightening skull. The laughter turned to roars. It took me a moment to take it all in. Our skull had been reshaped into a happy face. A round circle with those stupid slit eyes and mile-wide grin.

"How juvenile," someone snickered.

"Babyish," an eighth grader sneered. "Typical."

The kids cheered when I slammed off the power. Katelyn grabbed me. "Mike, what happened?"

"Someone must have sabotaged our display," I said.

Across the floor, Scott Schreiber smirked at me. Happy face or not, this Halloween dance was beginning to scare me.

We had planned our big show for halfway through the dance. I checked my laptop five times, making sure it was cabled correctly to the screen projector. Each time, my files were in order and everything was a go.

If only my heart could be electronically programmed. When the DJ slowed the music for the first close dance, I made up my mind to ask Katelyn right then. But by the time I got to her, she was already on the dance floor, in the arms of Scott Schreiber. *There's no chance for me,* I thought as I saw them together. Scott had it all—muscles, good hair, and a Hollywood-handsome face.

I went back to my computer and stayed there. I was safe amid my keyboard, mouse, and diskettes. But when the DJ slowed the music again, Katelyn came looking for me. "Let's dance," she said and took my hand. I hesitated.

"I'm not a good dancer," I stammered.

The music rose around us. Katelyn tugged at me. "What did you come for if you weren't going to dance?" She tugged at me again, and I was on the floor in a flash. And in a dream, with my arms around Katelyn and her head on my shoulder. Her heart beat against my chest, and I knew mine pounded like a drum. I stumbled a couple of times, but she kept me moving.

Then, too soon, the dance was over. Katelyn's dark eyes glimmered. "Thanks," she whispered.

I cleared my throat. It was now or never. "Katelyn?"

A blast of static cut my off my words. The DJ cleared the floor and nodded at us. Katelyn raised her eyebrows at me. "What?"

"Later," I said to Katelyn and trotted to the computer. I double-clicked on the pumpkin icon while Katelyn turned on the screen projector. The long wall filled with pure white light and all heads turned to it, waiting to see what would happen next. I pulled down the menu and clicked on PLAY.

The cafeteria filled with the Three Stooges and Looney Tunes. The riot of laughter started again.

"Mike!" Katelyn called. "Wrong file."

It was the right file! What went wrong? I typed and clicked and searched my hard drive. Meanwhile, the Stooges ran wild, bonking each other with frying pans. The Looney Tunes twittered at maximum volume.

This was not my creation.

Frankenstein, Dracula, and the Werewolf were right there before me, on my computer. Why weren't they on the wall? And where was "Ghoul's Night Out"? I ran to the cash register desk where the projector sat, protected from the crowd.

By Ryan and Terry, Scott's bullies.

"What the—?" I yelped. Meanwhile, the Stooges were freaking out, chasing each other with butter-fly nets. The crowd was getting bored.

"This is so juvenile."

"This isn't Halloween stuff."

"Who did all this stuff? Babies?"

My eyes followed the cables from the projector to a small table where Drew Mikalski sat at his own laptop computer, grinning. I lunged at him, but Scott Schreiber stepped out and grabbed me. Drew laughed then lifted his hand with a flourish and pressed the ENTER key.

The show resumed. This time all the Stooges wore my face. They—I—the Stooges—were in a pie-throwing contest. I was getting clobbered.

The laughter surged like an earthquake through the cafeteria. Scott Schreiber pointed at me and brayed.

All eyes turned to look at me, and then everyone knew who the biggest Stooge at the dance was.

I ran out the door, out of the school, and kept running.

9

SOME GENIUS I HAD TURNED OUT TO BE. I HAD always been the weird one, out of step with the world. What made me think that things could be different?

It was now very clear to me. Ashby Middle School was not the place for a kid like me. Dana and Pamela Pillsbury were not the parents for a kid like me. And Katelyn Sands was certainly not the girl for a kid like me.

There was only one way I would ever be happy.

I had to leave this planet.

The house was empty when I staggered home. My parents weren't expecting me until midnight and were off at some high-powered party. Jill was off with her obnoxious friends. Good—I needed peace and quiet.

I opened my computer and dug out the processor

chip and the hard drive. Then I grabbed a handful of cables and headed downstairs. In the family room, I unhooked the signal converter box from the TV. I carried everything into the kitchen where I jury-rigged a new converter, powered by a state-of-the-art processor and expandable RAM from my computer.

I took my device out to the backyard, where we have a nest of satellite dishes. One is for our TV, the others for my parents' jobs. I daisy-chained the dishes together, then cabled the cumulative signal through my device. I connected the device to my dad's transmitter box. Then I went to his office and fired up his computer system.

How best to get the message across? First, I pressed my hands on the photo scanner to record an image of my fingerprints. Then I pressed my face on the glass—both front and profile views. I went back to the computer and opened the electronic map file. I chose several views, including the Milky Way galaxy and our solar system. Then I focused on Earth, narrowing again and again until I had pinpointed Ashby.

I began to type.

Fellow citizens of the galaxy: I do not belong on this planet. I am being held against my will, trapped by ignorance and cruelty. You must save me. Take me away from this.

I am desperately in need of your assis-
tance. Please help me.
   Mike Pillsbury.

I electronically pasted the scans of my hands
and face and the map files into the document.
   I pulled down the File Menu and chose Send.
The dialog box listed the options: printer, fax, file
server. I scrolled past them to *unknown device*. My
device. I highlighted it, clicked OK.
   And I pressed the Send button.

   At first nothing happened. I sighed, fearing I
wasn't as smart as I hoped. "Come on," I whispered.
   Then the hard drive in my dad's computer
began to churn. The screen told me it was processing my request.
   I ran outside to the nest of satellite dishes. The
cables vibrated and the backyard hummed with
power. "Go," I said. "GO!"
   There was a surge of energy, and the satellite
dishes burst to life—whirring, clacking, glowing. I
had converted the signal so that instead of receiving,
the dishes would transmit. They were programmed to
send in unison, aimed at a communications satellite
orbiting two hundred miles over my head. When the
signal got to the satellite—if my programming
worked as I planned—it would magnify the signal
and send it to outer space.

I hoped.

"GO!" I shouted. "Tell them I need them!"

The satellites shook with a high-pitched whine. My ears tingled and I tried to rub out the buzzing. I had programmed a loop so the message would be sent over and over. The linkage between the dishes seemed to be creating a magnetic field, making my hair stand on end. The dishes glowed red and I stepped back.

"Please!" I cried. "Please, is someone listening?"

The whine increased to a resounding *thrum thrum thrum*. The cardboard box that held my device sparked, then flamed. I panicked at the barrage of energy I had released. The cables began to melt. I tried to disconnect the power but the cables were too hot. The satellite dishes howled as the signal surged through, over and over. The whole system glowed red, then white, then blue-hot.

Then, with a deafening *crack,* my backyard exploded.

10

Freak Lightning Strike, the weekend news-paper called it.

We had a crater the size of a school bus in my backyard. The satellite dishes were jumbled at the bottom in ashy remains. Only the elm tree and my treehouse were spared. My whole neighborhood was blacked out until Sunday afternoon.

Early Monday morning, work crews arrived to clean up the debris. I wondered who could clean up the debris of my life. What a mess I had made of everything. How could I be so weird as to think my fairy tales of Hanzels and Jongs were real? All I had succeeded in doing was blowing up my back-yard, proving once and for all how weird I was.

Mom and Dad sat over an early morning cup of espresso. The sunlight poured in through the bay window. Mom hugged me for the fortieth time since they had arrived home Friday night and found the disaster.

"Mom!"

"Just want to know you're okay," she said. "If that lightning had struck ten feet closer to the house . . ."

Dad ruffled my hair like I was a little kid.

"I told you I was okay," I mumbled. My parents were being so nice to me, I didn't have the heart to tell them that *I* was the cause of the freak lightning strike. "Mom and Dad, I've been thinking."

"Yes, Buck?" Dad asked, alert for whatever I had to say.

"Maybe I should change schools."

"Oh yes!" Mom said, aglow with the good news. "A private school would really challenge your talents."

"Bradford Military Academy," Dad pronounced.

Mom had her own ideas. "I was thinking the Varner School. They have an accelerated learning program."

Dad leaned over the table, ready to do battle. "Bradford has top academics. And rigorous physical training."

"But Varner offers cross-cultural studies. Corporate internships."

"A grueling physical environment would be just the thing the boy needs," Dad argued.

Their discussion faded as I grabbed my backpack and headed out the back door. Even Ashby Middle School, the Monday after my complete humiliation, would be better than what my parents could plan.

I crept toward my locker, willing myself to be invisible. Kids tromped around me, calling to each other, slamming lockers, dropping books. The warning bell rang, and I thought I just might make it to homeroom without notice when—

"Hey, Pillsbury!"

I buried my head in the locker. Someone grabbed me from behind and pulled me around. It was Ryan, Scott Schreiber's number-one bully.

"Hey," he said.

"Hey, what?" I said, waiting for the inevitable.

"Cool show," he said.

"Cool?"

"Yeah, cool," he said. The homeroom bell rang and he drifted away.

Was this some clever plan to humiliate me further?

In science class, out of habit, Katelyn slid into the next seat. She opened her book and pulled out her homework. She erased and wrote, erased and wrote.

There was a silence like lead: dark, hard, immovable. Katelyn twisted her hair around her fingers. I couldn't bear to look at her.

The silence weighed on my chest, pushing the air out of my lungs. I let an *ooooph* escape, halfway between a gasp and a sigh.

"What did you say?" Katelyn asked. She glanced quickly at me, her eyelids flickering.

"Nothing," I said. I chewed my thumb. It tasted like salt.

She threw down her pencil. "How come you wouldn't take my phone calls?"

"Huh?" I said. I was back to the one-word wonder.

"I tried to call you," Katelyn whispered. "But no one answered."

"The phone lines were down," I said. I stuck my nose in my book, staring at the picture of an opossum. A marsupial, the caption read. A rare form of mammal.

Like Mike Pillsbury.

"Oh," she said.

"Why did you call?" I asked before I could stop myself. The possum hung upside down from a tree.

"Because I was worried about you," she said. Then she turned to me with the smallest of smiles. I slammed my book shut. My throat tightened and tears dammed up in my eyes. Not now, please. I'd survived three days without tears. Let me go another five minutes.

"It was a stupid joke. No big deal."

I hid my head, wet eyes and all, under my folded arms. "Now everyone thinks I'm weird," I said through the crook made by my elbow.

"So what if they do?" Katelyn said. "Since when do you care what everyone thinks?"

"I don't care what everyone thinks. Just you." Then I closed my arms over my head and locked myself in, nice and tight.

11

NIGHT WAS FALLING AND AN EERIE STILLNESS HUNG
over the neighborhood. Halloween was only a couple
of days away. My parents weren't home from work yet;
I remembered something about a business dinner. As
I crossed toward the back door, I slipped and fell on
my backside into a disgusting puddle of—what?

Goo. Thick like butter, sticky like gum, stretchy
like taffy. I wiped my hands on my jeans, but the
stuff seemed to stick. The clean-up crew must have
left behind some nasty machine grease.

I left my gooey shoes on the back step. Inside,
I found a note in the kitchen.

Kids.
We'll be home around 10. Here's $20.
Get takeout.
Love, Mom and Dad.

Both Jill and the twenty dollars were missing.

I could live with macaroni and cheese. But first, I had to get rid of the goo. I scrubbed my hands with hot water and detergent, but the stuff was persistent. Under the light, it had a sparkle to it like purple threads laced in green sludge.

I headed up to my room, exhausted from laying low all day at school. Scott had avoided me. Everyone else acted like nothing had happened, talking about Halloween and the upcoming science fair. Katelyn gave me half-smiles all day, which only stirred my pain deeper.

I slipped again. More goo. I fumed as I headed for my bathroom to wash my hands. Had strangers been tromping through my room?

Strange doesn't even begin to describe what was lounging in my bathtub.

The thing was about four feet long and three feet wide—like a gooey worm with snaky arms.

But what worm would take a bath?

Someone else would have freaked. But I had imagined aliens all my life. An extraterrestrial stewing in my bathtub was a surprise, but not a bone-rattling shock.

"You came," I whispered. "You really came." And then I knew, without a doubt, without a fear, that I was okay. I wasn't a dreamer. I wasn't weird. I had been right all along, and the creature in my bathtub proved it.

The alien extended a tentacle at me. I willed myself to freeze. The tentacle snaked around my hand. It felt sandy and coarse under the thin coating of goo.

"You are the Pillsbury," the creature rumbled. Its words came from a small metal box hung at its upper torso.

"And you are?" I asked, wondering what the rules of galactic protocol were. My mom, who was an expert in international marketing, would probably know.

"I am a Bom," it said as it heaved itself out of the tub, wiggling to shake the water from its clumpy green body. "Excuse me for the water immersion, but I find your atmosphere rather arid."

"Not a problem," I assured it. "Where's your ship?"

The Bom emitted gas from the tiny orifices that ringed its belly. Laughter, I hoped. I held my nose anyway.

"A primitive concept," it said. It snapped the pointed ends of its tentacle, and a shining door appeared.

"A star gate," I said, awed.

"You are not as stupid as you look," the Bom said. "Shall we?" It tipped its head at the gate.

"Shall we what?" I asked.

"My apologies. I have misunderstood. You *are* stupid. Shall we leave?"

The phone rang. The Bom trembled at the sound, as if fingernails were raked on a chalkboard. "What is that racket?" it cried, beating its head with its tentacles.

"The phone," I said, trying to sound reassuring. "A primitive communication device."

It rang again. "Make it stop!" the Bom cried, sticking its snaky fingers into its ear holes.

I picked up the receiver. "Hello?" I said, still staring at the Bom.

"Hi."

"Katelyn," I said, watching the Bom as he crossed from the bathroom into my bedroom.

"Can I ask you something?" Katelyn said.

The Bom reached for my door. "Don't do that!" I yelled.

"Oh." Katelyn sounded hurt.

"Not you, Katelyn. The, ah . . ." I thought fast. "The plumber's here."

"We need to talk, Mike," Katelyn said. "About you and me."

The Bom slimed up my wall. "You and me?" It stuck to the ceiling, dripping goo. "Gross!" I yelped.

Katelyn gasped. "Gross what? You and me?"

"No. The . . . plumber. He's getting grease all over. I'm sorry, Katelyn. Where were we?"

"I was wondering if you thought it'd be a good idea . . ." she stopped.

"A good idea what?"

65

The Bom unscrewed the light bulb from the ceiling.

"If we tried to make a fresh start of things." She said it so fast I almost missed it.

The Bom was about to put its tentacle into the socket. "That's not a good idea!" I shouted.

"You don't have to be so brutal about it," Katelyn said. "I thought we were friends."

"Oh, no! You and me. That's a good idea." I was breathless. My world was moving too fast. "It's the electrician . . . he's about to . . ."

The Bom dropped with a hard *plop*. He crept across the floor and stuck his head out my window.

"I thought it was the plumber."

"Him, too. They're making a mess you wouldn't believe." Everything was so unreal—an alien in my bedroom, Katelyn on the phone, me in the middle. "Katelyn, I'm sorry I was such a jerk."

"You're not a jerk," Katelyn said. "So, I just wanted to make sure. We're still friends?"

"Yes!" I said. No hesitation. I jumped with glee and knocked the Bom through the window. "No!" I cried.

Katelyn was very patient. "If this isn't a good time . . ."

The Bom hung by a tentacle. I waved and he slimed up toward me. "Katelyn. It's a great time. Yes, we're still friends. A million times yes! No to this . . . guy . . . who's trashing my room."

"You'd better call me back," Katelyn said.

I couldn't let her go without making sure. "But we're okay, right? Friends."

"Maybe more than friends," she said and clicked off.

The Bom plopped back into my room. Now that his curiosity had been satisfied, he was all business.

"We must leave now."

How could I have forgotten? The Bom was there to take me away. Isn't that what I wanted?

I shook my head and breathed deeply, trying to clear my thoughts. "All my life, I waited for someone like you to come," I told him. "A real alien. A being from outer space."

The Bom emitted more gas. This time it was a huff, not a laugh. "I do not intend to wait all *my* life. Let us depart."

"No, no! This is unbelievable. First contact! I have to tell someone about you." I grabbed the phone. "Don't you want me to take you to our leaders? Talk to our scientists?"

The Bom ripped the phone from my hand. "This is a primitive planet. Off-limits to the rest of the galaxy. No contact is allowed."

"Then why did you come to me?" I asked.

"Your request to be rescued is a most intelligent one. That is the only reason I am here. That and my fee, of course."

"I'm afraid I can't pay you anything," I said.

"Not you. We will make *them* pay."

"Who's them?"

The Bom clicked his tentacle and a sparkling list of symbols appeared in front of his eyes. "The parties we will sue on your behalf. Starting with the earthlings, Pamela and Dana Pillsbury. We will get them for insufficient parenting. Then Nicholas Thorpe for improper peer support. Scott Schreiber for harassment. Katelyn Sands for alienation of affection. And then we will go after the Centurians and the Taureans and the . . ."

"Hey!" I yelled. "I never asked you to do any of this for me."

The Bom narrowed its breathing slit into what had to be a frown. "Your message was clear. You are in grave danger. You have a good case for removal from this planet."

"Circumstances have changed," I pleaded.

The Bom wrapped its tentacles around its head. "I do not want to hear it! You must remain the injured party!"

"I'm not injured. I don't intend to sue anyone. And I'm not sure I even want to leave this planet."

The Bom bristled with anger. "You unleash the powers of the galaxy and then dismiss them?"

"I made a mistake. I really am sorry."

"So you will not sue?"

"Never," I said.

"Will you at least vacate the planet?" the Bom huffed.

"I don't know. I need time to think about it."

"Do you know what my hourly rate is? You cannot afford *my* time," the Bom sneered.

"Then I have to say—" I hesitated. The gate glimmered in the middle of my room, an invitation to step into the unknown. The stars were open to me, beckoning me.

But so was Katelyn's offer—*more* than friends. "If I have to decide right now, I'd have to say no. I'm sorry."

"You think you are sorry now?" the Bom sneered. With a blast of foul gas, the Bom disappeared through its gate, pulling it in behind him as he went. For moments after he disappeared, his parting words lingered.

"Just wait."

12

I had to tell someone. I trusted Katelyn but I didn't want to stress our new friendship. So I called my oldest and best friend.

Three fans were blowing up a storm, trying to clear the stench from my room, when Nick arrived. I was on my hands and knees, up to my elbows in soap suds, trying to scrub the goo from my floor.

"What! What's the big surprise?" Nick said, then gagged. "Who barfed up your room?"

"It's not barf. It's—" How best to describe slime from outer space? "It's an emission," I said.

Nick gingerly fingered the sticky trail that criss-crossed my room. "From whose butt?" he grimaced.

I drew a deep breath. "I had a visitor," I said. "An alien."

Nick exploded with laughter. "You puked up your room just to play a joke?"

"This is no joke. An alien was here."

Nick stuck his head out the window and waved his arms. "Look, up in the sky! It's a bird! It's a plane! No, it's a UFO!"

"Ships are primitive," I sighed. "This alien used a star gate."

"Like that's original."

"It's the truth," I swore, soapy hand in the air, raised for an oath.

"The little kids could come up with a better story than this one," Nick sneered.

"It's true!"

"Yeah," Nick said. "And next you're gonna tell me you and Katelyn Sands are an item."

"We are," I said.

"You're pathetic," Nick said and left, slamming the door behind him. I sat there with my goo and soapsuds, confused and alone.

When I returned the cleaning stuff to the kitchen, my parents were there. Dad was grinding beans for gourmet coffee and Mom was getting the mugs.

"Ah, *Alberto Miguel. ¿Come te—?*" she began.

"I'm not in the mood," I snapped.

She glanced at my dad, then reassured me. "That's a valid emotion."

"How was football practice, Bu—Mike?" Dad asked.

"All right."

"Just all right?" Dad asked. Mom hushed him and he went back to grinding his beans. Mom hugged me.

"Mom, Dad. What if I were an alien?"

"Mike, we've heard your stories," Dad said. "They're great. But you're not an alien."

"How do you know!" I almost shouted.

"Because aliens just don't exist," Mom said in a quiet way. "Not on this planet at least."

Oh, if they only knew. Why couldn't they believe, when I believed so strongly? And now I knew for a certainty. Why was I so different from my family?

"Would you tell me if I were adopted?"

Dad cut power to the coffee grinder. It whirred to a whisper, then sputtered off. "Is football stressing you out?"

"Would you?" I asked.

"You know we believe in being open with you and Jill. If you were adopted, we would be just as happy to be your parents. But you are not adopted."

"Could I have been switched in the hospital?" I asked.

Dad began pacing the kitchen. Stove to sink to refrigerator, then back. Deep in thought. Finally he said, "Is it us?"

"This is normal adolescent behavior, Dana," my mother said. "Not wanting to be connected to one's parents. And stop that pacing, you're making us all more nervous than we are already."

"Nervous? Why is anyone nervous? Is it the lightning strike? Is that it?"

"You didn't answer my question," I said. My parents turned abruptly and stared at me.

"Why would you think you were switched at birth?" my mother asked.

"I'm not strong and aggressive like dad. I don't communicate easily like you, Mom. Maybe—you brought the wrong baby home."

My mother pulled me into a hug. I was taller than she was, but she felt strong and comforting. "From the instant you were born until we brought you home, you were not out of our sight," she said.

Dad wrapped his arms around mom and me. "Your mom held you all the time. Except when she was sleeping. Then I held you."

"Did you think someone would steal me or something?"

"We loved you so much, we couldn't bear to be parted from you," my mother said.

"Oh."

"For better or for worse, you're stuck with us," my father said.

"Oh. Okay."

"Is that all right, Mike?" my mother asked.

I hugged them back, hard. "If you don't mind, I don't mind," I said.

13

I KEPT MY MOUTH SHUT ABOUT THE BOM'S VISIT. I had a lot of stuff to figure out and for once, I wasn't the all-knowing genius. Did Katelyn and I have a future? Was there a place for me in seventh grade? Did everyone think I was weird, or was it just my imagination? And if they did, did it matter anyway?

Why make things worse with a wild story about some Jabba the Hutt in my bathtub?

Tuesday's football practice was a disaster. Maybe it was the full moon or the fact that Halloween was in a couple of days. We had lost our last two games and just couldn't get anything right. Coach Tremblay was ripping mad. "Come on, ladies. Keep screwin' up and Hawthorne's gonna eat your twinkies on Friday."

Scott threw his helmet down. "That last play just doesn't make sense."

"It's you that ain't got any sense, Schreiber," Coach barked. "Take a lap." Scott sprinted away, his anger steaming off him in waves. I knew he was mad at more than the coach. Some of the kids were angry with him, calling his stunt at the dance immature. Scott wasn't used to being odd man out, the role usually reserved for Mike Pillsbury.

"Coach?" I said.

"What? You wanna Q this team of Barbies?"

"No. I had an idea," I said. The coach just stared at me. I waited for him to order me to take a lap.

Then he sighed. "Okay, Pillsbury, let's hear it."

I took his play book. "How about if you tried this formation?" I said as I sketched.

His face brightened. "Not bad. Not bad at all."

Scott finished his lap and we all went to work.

After two months of football I wasn't much better at playing the game. But I had grown to respect it. The strategy, the play making, the use of resources—it was as stimulating as chess, but more exciting because the board pieces were flesh-and-blood players. I had been devising plays in my head for weeks now. That afternoon Coach let me run the team through a series of maneuvers. Some were disasters, but many were easy for the team to understand and execute.

An hour later, we looked like champions.

"What're we going to do to Hawthorne?" Coach roared.

"Kill!" we roared back.

Then it was off to the showers, our heads filled with visions of victory.

I walked home after practice. Jack-o-lanterns perched on every step, and white sheets with stuffed heads billowed ghostlike from lampposts. The moon, full and bright, was so big I imagined I could jump from the sidewalk right onto its face. *Tackle the moon,* I thought.

A wave of regret washed over me as I realized I could be out there, among the stars. I thought of Katelyn. Maybe the stars were right here on Earth.

Then I heard the rustling in the bushes.

"Who's there?" I called out.

Nothing.

I walked on, leaving the rustling behind me. I passed around the corner and through the small park, alert for moving shadows. I imagined ghosts jumping off the lampposts to chase me down the street. Pumpkins became sharp-teethed gargoyles, and orange lights strung on trees were bug-eyed monsters.

The wind whistled and the trees rained down their last few leaves. Dry and brown, they crunched underfoot as I picked up my pace.

As fast as I walked, I couldn't outrace the fear creeping up under my ribs. The bushes whispered, the leaves crackled, the wind sighed. Was something following me? Something bigger and meaner than a Bom? The Bom was gooey, but the Mantix had deadly slime. The Mantix had slime, but the Jongs had fierce weapons. No, I had made up the Mantix and Jong. But if the Bom was real, something else could be.

I passed by an oak stockade fence, strung with orange and white lights. Were there footsteps on the other side? No, just my own, echoing back at me. Wait. The pace wasn't quite right, the *clip clip* not keeping to my *clip clop*.

Time to run.

I shouldered my backpack and sprinted past the fence, past a yard with huge, barren lilac bushes, through a bright circle of light spread under a street lamp, and then into darkness.

I'm nuts, I told myself, making something out of nothing as usual. Thinking the whole world's against me. I stopped cold, shook the heebie-jeebies out of my head, and forced a little laugh.

"Nothing to be afraid of," I said out loud.

WHAMP! Some huge *thing* leapt in front of me. I screamed.

The *thing* laughed. "Scared, you little suck-up?"

"Shut up, Schreiber," I gasped.

"Your lips chapped from kissing coach's butt?" he said, pushing his face in mine.

I held my ground. "Did it ever occur to you that

all my plays make you look good?" No, it hadn't—
I could tell by the dull look in his eyes.

"You don't know anything about football," he
said, and shoved me against a tree.

"You don't know anything about anything. Get
out of my way." I pushed him back. He didn't
move much.

"Maybe I oughta knock some sense into you,"
he growled, and grabbed my jacket.

I grabbed his jacket and twisted it. "Maybe I
oughta knock some crap out of you," I squeaked.

There was more rustling. *Oh no,* I thought. *He's
got friends with him.* Scott cocked his fist back, and
I got ready to duck.

The bushes erupted. Something small and fast
hit Scott in the shoulder. He went down in a
thump, spinning me around as he fell.

The attacker was a poodle, yipping like the
world was coming to an end. Scott tried to get up,
but the poodle had his front paws on Scott's chest.
Super strength, I thought. Either that or Scott was
scared witless.

"Pillsbury. Help me!" he cried.

I laughed when I realized the poodle and I were
the only ones who had sacked Schreiber all season.

"PILLSBURY!"

I put my hand out to the dog. "Come on, doggie.
You don't want to bite that moron. You'll get food
poisoning . . . come on."

The dog gave me an odd look as if he understood. Then he backed off. Scott, sweaty and scared, rolled to his hands and knees, then pushed himself up. "Some day, Pillsbury . . ."

The dog growled. Scott ran like a madman, disappearing into the night.

I reached down to scratch the poodle's ears. His fur was gray and crisp. "I beg your pardon," he said in a starchy, formal voice.

"Huh?"

The poodle rose to its back legs, suddenly looking quite human. He had a small collar with a translator box, similar to the one the Bom wore.

"My people are offended by casual contact," he sniffed.

"Your . . . people?"

"My name is Barnabus. From the star system of Sirius."

"The dog star!" I exclaimed.

Even though the dog's head was two feet below me, he still managed to look down his nose at me. "An unfortunate coincidence, I assure you."

"My name is—"

"—the Pillsbury. I am here to rescue you."

"I'm sorry. I already told the other alien . . ." I began.

Barnabus clicked his teeth. "What other alien?"

"The Bom."

"A Bom. Notorious ambulance chasers," Barnabus said, his disapproval loud and clear.

"Huh?"

"The Boms sit by their galactic scanners, monitoring distress calls. Always out to profit from someone else's misfortune."

"So what do you do?" I asked.

"I represent a galactarian organization. Disaster relief, rights violations. Non-profit, of course."

"Of course."

Barnabus pointed his snout toward the center of town. "Shall we get on with the departure?" He dropped to all fours and trotted away.

"Wait. There's been a change . . . wait!" I yelled.

He followed me home.

After a polite but firm refusal, I had left him and headed for my house. But as I climbed my back step, he was there, waiting for me at the door. "I already told you, I'm not going with you," I whispered.

He trotted to the crater and sniffed. "And I am not leaving until I am convinced you are not in danger."

The spotlights came on. The back door opened and my perfect parents peered out. "How was practice, son?" Dad boomed.

"Great," I mumbled as I went in.

"You can share your feelings with us, Mike," Mom said, her voice warm but concerned.

"Honest, practice was great." I threw my backpack onto the table. Then stopped short at the *click, click, click.*

Barnabus had followed me in, trotting along on all fours like any poodle would do.

"Mike?" Mom said in her most diplomatic voice. "You didn't tell us you had company."

"Oh, great," I moaned.

"You should have told me you wanted a dog. We could have gotten a more suitable breed," Dad said. "Like a Rottweiler."

I opened the back door and pointed. "Out."

Barnabus sat and panted like any dumb dog.

"Fine," I snapped. "Two can play this game. Barnabus, meet my parents."

"Where did . . . Barnabus . . . come from?" Mom asked.

"Tell them," I said.

Barnabus barked. Mom was impressed. "How precious."

"Flea-bitten mutt. Tell the truth." Barnabus dropped his ears, curled his tail, and lay down. His sad eyes glistened from between his paws. "He's an alien," I said.

"Alien?" Dad asked. He couldn't hide his shocked look, and I knew he feared that his brilliant son had finally gone totally, over-the-edge nuts.

Mom forced a laugh. "I get it. *French* poodle? Alien. *Très bien, Albert.*"

I fumed. "Try alien from outer space. Who . . ."

I lifted Barnabus's ear and shouted, ". . . speaks perfect English."

My parents exchanged worried looks. "How . . . amusing," Mom said.

"Inventive," Dad agreed.

I shoved Barnabus. He rolled to his back and pedaled his paws in the air. My parents laughed. I shoved him again. This time he growled.

"Be careful," Dad warned. "We don't know if he's had shots."

"Get up and talk like a man," I shouted. Barnabus stood on his hind legs, curled his front paws in the beg position, and barked.

"He is clever," Mom said.

"You're not helping!" I screamed. He licked my hand. I bent down and whispered in his ear. "Please. I already told you. I want to stay here. You can go back to where you came from." Barnabus plopped down on his belly, head on paws. He wasn't going anywhere.

"Fine! Be like that!" I stormed out of the kitchen.

Mom called after me. "Alberto! What do we do with your . . . friend?"

"If he won't go back where he came from . . . send him to the dog pound!"

I had had my fill of pushy bullies and pushier aliens.

14

As usual, I was half asleep when I climbed onto the school bus the next morning. It wasn't until Terry poked me that I realized something was wrong.

"Who's the new guy?" Terry said.

As if in response, the driver turned and looked at me. He wore an elaborately braided ponytail and had a bushy brown beard. He had more chest hair sticking from the front of his shirt than even Coach Tremblay. His eyes were covered with bizarre purple sunglasses that wrapped all the way to his ears.

He had a familiar-looking box pinned to his jacket. A translator box.

"Who knows?" I shrugged.

At the next stop, I tried to slip out of my seat. *WHAP!* I was blocked by an invisible barrier. In front of me, Terry snoozed. Around and behind me, kids were talking or listening to tapes.

The driver kept his eye on the road. I sat back down and kept my eye on him.

When we got to school, everyone piled out. The barrier kept me in my seat. When the bus was empty, the barrier disappeared, and the driver motioned me forward. "Pillsbury. I'm here to take you away," he said in a voice as scratchy as his face.

"I told the others, I'm not going anywhere. Not right now, at least."

"What others?" the driver asked.

"The Bom and the Sirian."

The driver screeched. "The Bom's a snake. And the Sirian's a bleeding heart. I can get you the best deal."

"What deal?"

"An agency contract. Ten percent for me. You keep the rest."

"For doing what?" I asked.

The driver clapped his hairy hands. A glittering newspaper appeared in midair. It was a tabloid, titled *The Starlight*. The headline read:

INTELLIGENT LIFE DISCOVERED ON EARTH

My scanned face was pasted below.

"The intergalactic network is always looking for

new faces," the driver said. "True stories. Especially one as pathetic as yours."

I pushed open the door. "I'm not interested."

The driver jumped in front of me. "I didn't come all this way to take no for an answer."

"No."

"I'll drop my cut to seven-and-a-half percent."

"No!"

"Think of the babes," the driver leered.

I stared at his hairy body and thought. "Never!" I shouted.

I shoved past him and raced toward the school. He screeched after me, "Pillsbury! You coulda been somebody!"

Inside the school building, I struggled to open my locker, paranoid that some swamp thing would grab me from behind. When something tapped my shoulder I jumped, smashing my face against the metal door.

"Hey." It was Katelyn. "Calm down."

"Hey."

Kids walking by did doubletakes. Katelyn leaned against my shoulder, making us a very public *couple*. Sarah Noyes smiled at me. "Hi, Mike. Hi, Katelyn."

Ryan stopped and punched my arm. "How's it goin', Mike?" It was as if everyone knew some secret. And then I realized Katelyn was smiling at me. No one else, just me.

And I knew the secret.

"Still friends?" I whispered.

"More than friends," she whispered back.

I yanked open my locker. Something tickled my hand and I turned fast. Inside was a pink blob, with a multitude of eyes waving on stalks. I slammed the door.

"What's the matter?" Katelyn asked.

"I . . . forgot my math homework," I stammered. A stalk poked through a vent in the door. I slapped my hand over it. It grazed my palm and I prayed, *please let it be friendly*.

Katelyn sniffed. "Do you smell that?"

"No!" I yelled, then recovered. "Smell what?"

She wrinkled her nose. "Like very expensive perfume." She sniffed the locker next to mine, then mine. "You're not hiding something, are you?"

I faked a laugh. "What would I be hiding?"

"Why does your locker smell so pretty?"

"Kids are always playing jokes on me," I said. "You know that."

The bell rang. "I'm late for homeroom," Katelyn said, trying to hide the suspicion in her eyes. She walked away, then turned back. "There's—there's not someone else, is there?"

"No. Of course not."

She smiled and left.

I opened my locker a crack. An eye poked out. The pink blob began to creep to the outside of my locker.

"Holy crap! Of all places, not here!" I whispered. I tried to shove it back in. Warm and smooth, it flowed all over my hand.

Heavy footsteps tromped down the hall. I scraped the blob off my hand and rolled it into a ball, hiding all its eyes.

"Mr. Pillsbury! You're late," boomed Principal Goodrich.

"I'm sorry. I had some trouble with my locker," I stammered.

"What's that?" Mr. Goodrich asked. We both stared at the pink blob in my hand.

"Would you believe . . . an alien?" I said in a small voice.

"Would you believe a detention?" Mr. Goodrich snapped. "If you don't cut the storytelling."

I sighed. "Bubblegum."

Mr. Goodrich ripped a hall pass from his pad and held it out to me. I just stood there. "Now, Mr. Pillsbury."

I plopped the blob onto the paper. Mr. Goodrich folded the pass and stuffed it in his pocket. "Get to homeroom."

I trotted away. "Mr. Pillsbury?" he called after me.

"Yes, sir?"

"No more of this pink stuff in school," he warned.

We could only hope.

15

KATELYN CAME HOME WITH ME AFTER SCHOOL to work on a science project. I made cocoa and peanut butter crackers while Katelyn poked around the kitchen. She paused at the bay window overlooking our backyard.

"This is the famous lightning strike?" she asked.

I steadied my voice. "Yep."

"Wow," she said. "What a mess." Then she leaned out, looking toward the tree. "Killer tree-house. Looks like a spaceship."

I carried our snack to the table. "Yeah. I spend . . . I used to spend . . . a lot of time up there."

"It looks so real," Katelyn said.

"You don't think playing spaceship is weird?" I asked.

"No. Sounds like fun."

"Some kids might think—"

89

"So what," she said.

Yeah, so what.

Jill stormed into the kitchen. She paused in front of Katelyn. I could tell by her blank look that my sister had forgotten she was in charge while our parents were at work.

"Hey, Albert. You left something on in your room. TV or something. I can't study," she said.

"So shut it off," I replied.

"I'm not going in there. Your room stinks."

I jumped out of my chair, picturing my room filled with an army of Boms. "I'll be right back."

It was far more spectacular than even I could have imagined.

A menagerie of aliens greeted me. A slender one with billowy wings introduced herself, then the others. Lula resembled a five-foot-tall butterfly. Her torso was covered with dark fuzz and had tiny arms and legs. Her wings floated behind her in marigold colors of yellow and red. She was a vision of beauty but her translator box made her sound like a Brooklyn truck driver.

The Jarm had a humanoid body covered with muddy brown fur. His head had four faces, each one showing a different personality.

The Roswell was just what you see in all the tabloids—pasty white and smooth-skinned. His oversized oval head perched on his long, narrow neck. His eyes were large and liquid, and he blinked frequently.

A steaming glass tank sat in the middle of my room, as high as my bunk bed. Lula introduced the blob swimming in the milky gray fluid as the Judge.

The Jarm took four turns around me so each of its faces could have a good look. Then JarmOne snickered, just like Nick at his finest. "We came all this way for a hairless lump?"

The Roswell hiccuped. "Whatever is wrong with hairless?"

JarmTwo cried real tears. Purple tears. "Show some compassion."

JarmThree agreed. "Its desperation couldn't be ignored."

JarmFour laughed. "Nor can its smell." All four Jarm noses wrinkled.

Lula waved a stained glass wing at me. "We come to take ya away."

I thought of Katelyn downstairs, sitting over the steaming cocoa. I thought of Coach Tremblay and his new book of plays. I thought of my parents, who strove to be perfect so their children could be. I even thought of snickering Nick. I wanted to go so much it hurt, but I wanted to stay so much it hurt.

"Thank you, I really appreciate the offer. But could we delay the departure?"

"For how long?" the Roswell asked.

I gulped and replied as politely as possible. "Perhaps seven or eight Earth years?"

Lula's antennae shot sparks. The Roswell dived under my bed.

"It's now or never, buddy," Lula snarled.

"I can't go now," I said. I bowed my head with respect just like I've seen my mother do with her Asian clients. "So perhaps it must be—" I could barely say the word "—never."

"These are your words, buddy," Lula said. "Listen up: *I am being held against my will, trapped by ignorance and cruelty. Take me away from this.* Am I hearin' dis right?"

I stuttered, "Yes, but . . ."

"But what?" she snarled.

"As I explained to the others," I said, trying to imitate my mother's diplomatic tones. "I changed my mind."

JarmOne blinked. "I can identify with that." JarmTwo, Three, and Four agreed.

The Judge's tank bubbled. Something fleshy and green pressed against the inside of the tank, gaping like a demented trout.

The Roswell peeked out from under my bed. "Now you've done it," he squeaked.

"Done what?" I asked.

"Ticked off da Judge," Lula said.

"I'm sorry," I said.

JarmOne blinked. "He's sorry?"

JarmTwo said, "He's not the one who traveled seventeen light years . . ."

". . . expecting to be a hero . . . " JarmThree continued.

". . . and ending up a fool," JarmFour finished.

Lula folded her wings and crossed her front torso with them. Now she looked like a rabid bat. "You're in deep doo-doo, Pillsbury. Dere's bad, bad penalties for false alarms."

"Penalties?" I gulped.

The Roswell popped its huge eyes at me. Then he took his long, bony finger and slashed it across his throat.

"The Judge is gonna order us to fry you," Lula said.

Each of the Jarms agreed. "Fry, fry, fry, fry!"

"I don't understand," I cried. The sweat poured down my back. This was worse that facing ten Scott Schreibers. "What did I do wrong?"

Lula stamped her appendage. "Ya cried for help. The whole galaxy heard ya, and anyone with an ounce of mercy came to help ya. And now ya blow us off?"

The tank trembled. The Judge spoke in a clear, horrible voice. "Flagrant disregard of galactic compassion is punishable by death."

I wanted to run. But if they could jump light years in a day, they could find me anywhere. I had to stand my ground. Worse, I had to face the Judge, make him understand. I forced myself toward the tank. The Judge moved and through the swirling haze I saw his teeth, pointed and razor-sharp.

Not like a trout, I thought. *A shark.*

I pressed my face against the glass. "Please understand, sir," I begged. "I never thought anyone would actually answer."

The Jarm didn't care. "Fry, fry, fry, fry," he cried. I wanted to slap all four faces.

The Judge whirled to face them. The fluid in his tank flamed like lava. "I am the Law!" he barked. The Jarm slinked to a corner.

"Plead your case, Pillsbury," the Judge ordered.

Most of me wanted to faint dead away. But a small, deep part of me took joy in being so close to this incredible alien. Even if he could sentence me to death.

I spoke from my heart. "I thought I couldn't survive here. I am young and foolish and have a lot to learn. I guess I'm not as smart as I thought I was."

The Roswell crept toward me. "Let's take out his brain and see."

"Silence!" the Judge roared.

I fell backward, stunned. My stomach turned over and a sharp pain knifed through me. *This is what terror feels like,* I thought.

I forced myself back to the tank. "I realized that . . . not only can I survive . . . but I belong here. I have wanted all my life to travel the stars.

To see wonderful sights. To know all of you. But now is not the right time. "I am terribly sorry for taking your time. I certainly intended no disrespect or disregard."

The Judge pressed his full face against the glass—bulging eyes, jagged teeth, thick skin filled with knobs and crannies and orifices. But I could see wisdom in the ugliness. He had the face of one who had traveled far and learned well.

All the creatures quieted to hear his pronouncement. "Federation law allows one act of mercy. You are pardoned. Do not let it happen again."

"I won't. I promise, Judge sir. I promise," I swore.

"You are never to contact us again. The consequences will be dire," he finished. Then he spoke to his colleagues. "Vacate the premises."

In a blinding flash, the Judge's tank disappeared.

The Jarm shook open a transponder. "Beam me up, Scottie," JarmOne said. JarmTwo winked as they dematerialized.

The Roswell snapped his fingers and a star gate appeared. He passed through, taking the gate with him.

Lula perched on my window sill. "I hope ya ain't opened a can of woims," she said.

"Woims?" I said, wondering if they were like Boms.

"Woims," she growled. "Can of woims."

"Oh, worms!"

"Yeah, woims."

"What do you mean?" I asked.

"Your false alarm is bouncin' all over the galaxy. Others might come . . . others not as nice as us."

She leapt from the window and drifted over Jay's house, spreading her colored wings like a rainbow in the falling dusk. Then a flash and she was gone, zooming into the sky. I watched the trail of sparks she left in the deep blue. I had to wonder how the world looked from up there, how all the worlds of this galaxy could look, if I had chosen to go.

Now I would never know.

I sat in my room for a few minutes, thinking about the decision I had made. My belly was churning with regret about what I would miss and hope at what good things could happen for me here. Beginning with Katelyn, who, I suddenly remembered, was waiting for me downstairs.

I went to the window to shut it. Something moved below me in the yard. Katelyn skirted the crater and headed for the elm tree. I enjoyed watching her, happy that she was there with me.

She climbed the ladder to my treehouse, moving with grace and confidence up each rung. Up into the tree limbs. And then, I realized with horror—

up to the spacecraft that hovered above my treehouse.

Not the spaceship Nick and I had made with wood and nails and foil.

This was the real thing!

16

Coach Tremblay and Dana Pillsbury would have been proud at how fast I moved. I was downstairs, out of the house, and up the ladder in under sixty seconds.

The spacecraft was shiny and silver, about the size of a station wagon. It was smooth and simple but had an aura of power—nothing to mess with.

"Katelyn!" I yelled as I pushed through the leaves.

She looked down at me with a bright smile. "I knew you were smart, but this is so incredible."

She was three rungs away from the tiny entrance at the base of the ship. I grabbed her foot. "Don't go in there!"

She tugged away and stepped up another rung. "Don't tell me it's off limits to girls."

"It's not that . . ."

"Great." And she disappeared inside.

The entrance port was a narrow hall. "Katelyn?" I called.

"Mike?" Her voice trembled. I turned a sleek corner and found her.

She was staring at a miracle.

How could this be? The ship was no bigger than my Dad's minivan. But in front of us was a vast, open chamber—at least two hundred feet wide and a thousand feet above and below. It was crossed with wide beams of light and honeycombed with doors to hallways similar to the port from which we had come.

Katelyn's eyes were glassy. Her face was white and her skin was ice cold. "It's okay, Katelyn," I said, rubbing her hands in mine.

"What is this?" she whispered.

"The real thing."

She gulped in air, but still couldn't force more than the tiniest of voices. "A spaceship?" she said.

"A spaceship," I said, letting the wonder of it all wash over me in waves.

As if in a trance, Katelyn stepped forward onto a light beam. "How could something so small be so big?"

"We can't even dream of all the possibilities," I said. "I assume these guys have discovered a way to fold and unfold space to make more efficient use of it."

Katelyn looked down. I grabbed her before she fell.

"We'll go back," I said.

Below us, hundreds of light beams intersected the chamber. At the bottom were deep shadows and the distant purr of engines. Ahead of us and on all sides were the open halls, beckoning into darkness. Katelyn took it all in.

"No. No." She breathed deeply and now her voice was strong. "We'll move forward."

"Wait." I took the scrunchie ribbon from her ponytail and twisted it around a knob at the port where we entered.

She grinned. "You're so smart. You think of everything."

I hoped I wasn't too smart for my own good.

As we walked, we saw spectacular sights, things even I had never dreamed of—everything except the owners of the ship.

The first room was a cozy cafeteria. Pictures of foodstuffs lined a long wall. We yukked at most of them, bizarre menu items like squirming spinach and crusty rocks.

Katelyn touched a picture of an all-American hamburger. A tray slid from the wall, complete with burger and fries. She raised her eyebrows at me so I picked up the burger. It smelled barbecue-delicious and I couldn't resist. I opened my mouth for a big bite.

It moved!

I shoved it back onto the tray. Uneaten.

A playroom was next—a huge, round area filled with throwing toys resembling balls, boomerangs, Frisbees, and footballs. Katelyn tossed up an orange rubber ball.

We counted a full minute as it hovered in the air. It didn't come back down.

I spiraled a football and watched it pass back and forth over my head. We filled the air with spinning, twisting, flying missiles. Then Katelyn threw the boomerang. It chased her around the room and we dived out into the hall.

My favorite stop was the map room. With the flick of a wand, the universe filled the room in three-dimensional splendor, complete with grids and coordinates. We clicked and pointed until we found the Milky Way. Then we walked hand-in-hand through the friendly stars.

Katelyn discovered an art gallery with pictures of exotic scenes. One wall was filled with paintings of what appeared to be alien conquests. Katelyn was fascinated with the portrayal of a legion of rat-faced soldiers, armed with laser sabers. *The Mantix,* I thought. But this was no Hanzel Chronicle, dreamed up in my treehouse. This was really happening.

Katelyn pressed the button next to the painting and the room filled with marching and grunting rat soldiers. They lifted their sabers and signaled an attack. Katelyn screamed and I dove for the button. Another press and they disappeared.

We made another hasty exit, this time back to the center chamber. "Where do you think they are?" Katelyn asked.

"Who?" I asked, still fretting about the rat beasts.

"The people—aliens—who own this ship."

Time for the truth. "Out looking for me."

"Why would they look for you, Mike?"

I took her hand and looked into her trusting eyes. "Katelyn. How weird can I be and still have you like me?"

"I like you a lot," she said. "So I guess you can be a lot weird."

I told her the truth. The whole truth.

When I finished, she rubbed her eyes, hard. I held my breath as she blinked out the surprise and shock of the story. She shook her head to clear it and sighed. "Weird," she said.

Then she smiled. "But pretty darn awesome."

We had been there almost an hour. Common sense said *get out* but we were reluctant to leave. We decided to explore one more room.

"It's dark in here," Katelyn said. As if in response, the room lit slowly. It was large and circular, with built-in displays behind transparent panels.

The first display opened into acres of barren landscape, as if we were peering into another land. "I still can't get over how they do that," Katelyn said. "How they bend space." Fire spouts erupted and a flame-breathing, rocky-skinned creature appeared. Katelyn reached for the button next to the display.

"Don't do that!" I yelped, remembering the rat soldiers.

She grinned and pressed it anyway. A speaker garbled sounds at us.

"I beg your pardon?" Katelyn said.

The speaker responded, "Earthbound English." It began a canned spiel: "The Xgonearks are natives of the solar system Betelgeuse. Their organic chemistry is silicon-based. . . ."

Amazing.

We went to the next panel. Even though it wasn't more than ten feet from the first display, it opened into acres of red-grassed meadows, filled with prancing unicorns. I pressed the speaker button. "The Lopers are natives of the solar system Aries. They have a long history of . . ."

Katelyn and I drifted apart, fascinated by all the creatures.

And then I saw a display that made my blood

run cold. I couldn't move, couldn't speak. I just stared.

Katelyn skipped toward me. "Mike! This is incredible! It's a giant zoo!" She stopped cold when she realized what I was staring at.

Behind the panel were my yard and house.

"And I'm the next monkey," I mumbled.

17

"You're making a big deal out of nothing," Katelyn said. I dragged her along a walkway on the perimeter of the cavern. Where was the scrunchied port? "Why do you always have to do that?"

"You saw the display," I argued.

"You said the other aliens wanted to help you," Katelyn said, trying to calm me. "The display is meant to make you feel at home."

"The display is meant to *be* my home." There it was, about four levels down and directly across. I yanked Katelyn onto a ramp.

"Mike Pillsbury, the whole world is not out to get you," she said, pinching my arm. We were halfway down the ramp when something stepped in front of us.

A Jong!

He reared up in front of us, with the cobra head, strong arms, and many feet. "Good day," he said.

My heart stuck in my throat. I backpedaled and tripped.

Perhaps it had been a trick of light. He was no Jong; instead, he was quite human, tall and well-muscled. His face was handsome and his smile pleasant. Besides, the Jongs were simply a product of my imagination.

I hoped.

This person seemed kind and welcoming. And yet—what about the display? My cage?

"I'm not going to hurt you," he said, extending a hand to help me up. I crept backwards. Katelyn grabbed my arm and pulled me up.

"Stop it," she whispered. "Now you are being weird."

The alien nodded. "I understand, this is all new to you."

Katelyn assumed her class president voice. "It's very impressive." She extended her hand and he shook it, like any polite Earth person would. "My name is Katelyn Sands, and this is Mike Pillsbury."

My gut churned. "He wants to kidnap me," I whispered.

Katelyn gave me a sharp look. "Weird AND paranoid," she whispered. Then, back to the alien. "I hope you'll excuse our . . . intrusion . . . but no one was home."

He bowed. "I'm pleased you stopped in. I am Lord Blade, from the constellation of Ophiuchus."

Ophiuchus? That name jogged something loose in my muddled brain. "We really must leave," I urged.

"There's no hurry," Blade said. "Is there?"

Katelyn had stars in her eyes. Sure, the alien was dashing and handsome and a lord. But . . . Ophiuchus? What kind of place was that? I ran the constellations through my mind, trying to remember. Aquarius, the water bearer. Leo, the lion.

"We have homework," I stuttered.

"I think our teachers will understand," Katelyn replied. She couldn't take her eyes off Lord Blade.

I visualized the night sky. Orion, the hunter. Draco, the dragon. Where was Ophiuchus? And what was Ophiuchus?

Blade swept his arm at the expanse of ship. "Think of what you can learn here!"

Aries, the ram. So many constellations. What was it about Blade's home system that irked me? Lepus, the rabbit. Taurus, the bull.

Though his demeanor was calm, almost gentle, there was something about his eyes. Restless. Flicking about to watch every corner.

And then, it hit me. "OPHIUCHUS! The constellation of the serpent bearer!"

"Smart boy," Blade said.

"Smart enough to know who you really are!" I

yelled. I knew, more deeply than I've ever known anything. "Jong!"

Blade's facade crumbled. His smile transformed into a fanged mouth, his laughter into hissing. His shoulders flared into a hood and his body sprouted muscular arms.

A Jong. Once he existed only in my Chronicles; now we were face-to-face.

Katelyn screamed. Her dashing knight had transformed into a nightmare.

"Come on!" I shouted. We dashed across the light beam to the other side, still two levels up and a right angle from our exit. We aimed for a down ramp as Blade looped himself over the railing, bending and arching like a tree snake.

He dangled before us, his tongue flicking and his eyes gleaming. We jumped onto another light beam. Blade stood upright, unsheathed a laser gun, and cut our beam. We tottered over the darkness.

"Mike!" Katelyn cried.

I pulled her back. Blade cut the beam on our other side, stranding us in midair, with only ten feet of light beam between us and certain death— an island of light in a sea of horrors.

Blade chipped away at our beam, teasing us. Our foothold shrunk to nine feet, then eight, smaller and smaller until Katelyn and I clung to each other with only a patch of light under our feet. Blade waved his laser under our little island and it began to rock. Up, down, up a little higher, down a little lower. In seconds we would be tossed off.

Suddenly there was a wild barking at the exit port.

"Barnabus!" I yelled.

"Who's Barnabus?" Katelyn asked, holding to me for dear life.

"Man's best friend," I said.

Barnabus ran out of the light beam two levels below us. "Jump!" he called. "Jump! Now!" Was he crazy?

Blade hissed and dropped down a beam. He hung above us.

"Jump!" Barnabus barked. "Jump! It's your only hope!"

"What do we do?" Katelyn trembled in my arms. Blade's tongue flicked at our heads. I held her tight.

And jumped.

We flew through the first light beam as if it weren't there. But when we hit the one Barnabus was on, it was solid. The beam undulated like a rubber ribbon, bouncing up and down, up and down. The three of us scrambled to keep our balance.

"Run!" Barnabus yelled.

Katelyn reached the exit first. Barnabus and I were almost there when Blade lasered the beam before us. Barnabus didn't hesitate—he leapt the void and clawed onto the walkway.

Katelyn held out her hands to me. "Jump, Mike, jump!"

Blade lasered off another foot. The gap was at least eight feet.

"Now!" Barnabus barked.

The darkness stretched below me like Blade's dark eyes—dangerous and unyielding.

I backed up a few feet to get a running start.

Then I jumped.

We ran into the kitchen, breathless. My parents drank their after-dinner cappuccino from china cups.

"You must be Katelyn," my mother said with a welcoming smile.

"Yeah," Katelyn panted. My parents, living in their perfect world, didn't notice the panic in her face.

"Out running around, kids?" Dad asked.

"Mike," Katelyn gasped. I squeezed her hand in warning. She dropped her voice. "Shouldn't we tell them?"

I whispered back. "They'll think we're nuts. They don't believe in aliens. They only believe in the bottom line."

"Mike?" Dad continued, waiting for a response. "Why the big hurry?"

"We were jogging. Katelyn plays field hockey."

Dad beamed his approval. "Wonderful!"

Barnabus walked in, then dropped to all fours when he saw my parents. "The dog's back," Mom noted.

All eyes were on Barnabus. He sat pretty in the middle of the kitchen. "Mike. We can get you something with a pedigree," Mom offered.

"A Doberman, perhaps," Dad added.

I put my arms around Barnabus. He stiffened under my casual contact. "I'm keeping him."

Outside there was a crack of thunder. Startled, I ran to the window.

"Don't worry, darling," Mom said. "Lightning won't strike the same place twice."

Violet lights whirled through the leaves. Blade's ship rose slowly into the night, out of sight. I sighed with relief. Katelyn sank into a chair and rubbed her eyes.

Jill picked that moment to make her entrance. She gave me an ornery look. "Here you are."

"Brilliant observation," I said.

"That little nit Jay was just looking for you."

I grimaced. "It's past his bedtime. Did you send him home?"

Jill shook her head. "I thought you were still up in the treehouse so I sent him out there."

The treehouse!

*   *   *

111

I raced up the ladder. Barnabus and Katelyn waited at the foot of the tree.

The evening was quiet and cold. Blade's blast-off had shaken the last of the leaves from the tree, but otherwise it was as if the ship had never been there. Everything was in its place—cartons of books, boxes of paper and markers, stashes of snacks. The foil blanket was neatly folded and stuffed under a bench. Everything looked fine. We were worried about nothing.

I moved back to the ladder to go back down. Crunch. Something broke under my foot. I held the twisted plastic debris up to the backyard light, straining to see.

Jay's glasses.

18

WE RAN THROUGH THE NEIGHBORHOOD, SEARCHING for Jay. "We have to tell someone," Katelyn gasped. "The police. The army. Someone."

"You can't do that," Barnabus said.

A light flashed overhead. We dived into the bushes and huddled in the shadows.

"Why not?" I asked. Jay's parents thought their five-year-old was safe in bed. What would happen when they went to get him up for kindergarten and found him missing? By the time they went looking for him, he might be light years away.

Barnabus explained. "Earth is off-limits to all extraterrestrial contact until the planet completes its development."

"But you came for me!" I said.

"The ban was lifted temporarily so you could be rescued. Giving Blade the legal loophole he needed to come to Earth and collect another specimen."

"A can of worms," I moaned. "I opened a can of worms."

"Once contact is made, the Galactic Federation has to decide whether Earth can be admitted to the membership."

Katelyn shrugged. "So?"

Barnabus sighed. "You still have too many wars, too much cruelty on this planet. You are not ready to take your place in the galaxy."

"But a creep like Blade gets to be a member?" I yelled.

"Shush!" Katelyn slapped her hands over my mouth. "What if he hears you?"

"His people were the reason we tightened the rules," Barnabus explained.

I pushed Katelyn's hands off my face. "So we get rejected? So what?"

"It's more than rejection. This planet would have to be . . ." Barnabus paused. Even with the translator, I could feel his pain. "This planet would have to be neutralized."

"Neutralized?" Katelyn asked. "And that process would be . . . ?"

"Don't ask," I said. "Just don't ask."

Minutes later, Barnabus led us to a used car lot near Ashby center. In the back row, we approached a trashed minivan. Barnabus pawed at his collar and a ramp extended from the side door.

Unlike Blade's ship, Barnabus's ship was exactly what it seemed—cramped. No folding and unfolding space in this wreck. Barnabus dug through a cargo chest and came up with a device marked with a circle and cross.

"We have to get Jay back on our own?" I asked.

"I'm afraid so."

Katelyn picked up what looked to be a communicator. "Why don't we just call out there for help?"

Barnabus and I leapt for the microphone. "I've been warned," I said. "No more long-distance calling."

"It's hopeless then." Katelyn sighed. "You saw his ship. Blade's gone by now."

Barnabus shook his head. "He won't leave until he has a female specimen. He needs a pair."

"Great," I said. "He'll just pick some innocent person off the street."

"No. To make it legal, it has to be a female who is connected to you."

I shuddered to think of it. "My mom. Or my sister."

Katelyn's face froze. "Or me." She grabbed my hand. "Mike. How weird can I be and still have you like me?"

It was a crazy plan but what choice did we have? My parents thought I would be at Nick's for the night and Katelyn's parents believed she was at Sarah's. We hated to lie, but the truth could bring destruction to the whole planet.

I packed a bag, tossing in my laptop, cables, and some special diskettes.

"This is too dangerous," Barnabus warned.

"We can't let that creep Blade get away with this," I said.

"There's only three of us. We won't pull this off. The Jongs are known throughout the galaxy for their brutality. Their vicious, cruel ways."

"I know," I said. And wondered for a moment, how did I know?

Katelyn said, "We could get some friends to help us."

"No!" Barnabus snapped. "Any contact is strictly against galactic law. Unless you know someone who has had an accidental physical contact with an extraterrestrial."

I did.

I would have more likely expected to find myself on Mars than outside Scott Schreiber's bedroom window in the middle of the night. But these were desperate times.

I shone a flashlight through the glass. His walls were decorated with posters of sports heroes and big women in little bikinis. I slid open the window and Scott awoke in a sudden panic, the light bright on his sleepy face.

"Pillsbury. I'm gonna rip your head off."

"I got a better idea," I said.

"What could be better than tearing you into a million pieces and flushing you down the can?" he growled.

"How would you like to prove just how tough you are, Schreiber?" I challenged.

He tossed the covers off and sat up. His chest swelled and his face lit with pride. "Man, I can be tougher than anyone in the world," he boasted.

"What about out of this world?" I asked.

19

"WHY SHOULD I HELP YOU?" SCOTT HOWLED as we dragged him down the sidewalk. "Other than I'm the strongest, toughest kid you know."

It was time to settle this once and for all. I stepped in front of him and stared him down. "Because we're on the same side. Same football team, same school, same town. Same planet. We've got to stop picking at each other, wasting our time. We've got to work together."

Scott stared back. His eyebrows twitched and I realized he was considering the wisdom of what I had said. "It's the only way we can really win, Scott."

"This doesn't sound like a game, Pillsbury."

"That's why we need all the good men—" As soon as the words were out of my mouth, Barnabus growled and Katelyn groaned. I corrected myself. "—folks we can get."

Scott nodded. He was eager to prove himself, eager to find glory. But even more so, he was fascinated by Barnabus.

"A talking dog. I can't believe it," he said, over and over. "Man oh man, awesome. A talking dog, man. Man—"

"Stop it!" Barnabus nipped. "I am not a man. I am not a dog. I am a Sirian."

"Isn't that like in the Middle East?" Scott asked.

"A little farther than that." I sighed.

Within minutes we were in the field house on the Ashby football field. It was locked up tight. "What do we do now?" I said.

"Hut," Scott barked and threw his shoulder into the door. It sprang open and we were inside in seconds.

"See, smart doesn't get you everything," Scott gloated.

I cabled my laptop to the panel that controlled the electronic scoreboard. Even with the threat to Jay, I couldn't help but feel jazzed. Running the scoreboard would be like playing with the world's biggest computer.

The scoreboard buzzed to life, a shimmering gray. I clicked my mouse and the board filled with Katelyn's picture. Magnified many times, she was more beautiful than ever. I added a border of flashing red and white lights to make her picture more noticeable.

Katelyn reached for the mike to the public address system. I touched her hand.

"You don't have do this," I said.

She mustered a brave smile. "You think I can't keep up with you football jocks?" Her hand shook as she fumbled with the On switch. The field whined with feedback and then her voice came through, perfectly clear.

"Lord Blade, this is Katelyn Sands. Mike Pillsbury is holding me against my will. I want to go with you. I beg you to come rescue me."

She repeated it several times, then clicked off the mike. "Now what?"

"We wait," Barnabus said.

We fell silent. I adjusted Katelyn's picture to make her pretty face brighter. What was I doing, bringing this awesome girl into my weird life? Exposing her to horrible dangers? "Katelyn," I began again. "You don't have—"

"Enough already," she snapped. "Why should you have all the fun?"

Barnabus watched the skies. Scott bit his nails. "So how big is this Blade guy?"

"Scared?" I asked. My insides were quivering but my hands and voice were steady.

"Bug off, Pillsbury. I just want to be prepared."

"He's a snaky kind of guy," I said. "No muscles to speak of."

Scott flexed his biceps. "Loser," he sneered.

Out of the night sky came a *whirring,* followed by a moving violet light.

"An unidentified flying object!" Scott shouted.

"That's no UFO," I corrected. "We know exactly who it is."

"And what he wants," Katelyn shuddered.

Blade's ship landed at the far goalposts.

"Holy crap on a bun!" Scott gasped.

"Time to bait the trap," Barnabus said.

I grabbed my shoulder pads and helmet. Scott was cemented to the floor, staring. "Move it!" I yelled.

Scott grabbed his equipment and we ran into the darkness under the bleachers.

Katelyn sat under a spotlight in the middle of the stands. She whistled a bold tune but her feet tapped out a nervous cadence. Footsteps padded in the grass, heading downfield.

"Lord Blade?" Katelyn asked.

"Katelyn. You're making a wise decision." Blade stepped into the spotlight. Wearing his human facade, he looked like an intergalactic hero.

"I really want to go," Katelyn said. "But I'm nervous about being alone."

"You'll have a friend to keep you company."

"What friend?"

Blade smiled. "A little man named Jay."

"Is he on the ship?" Katelyn asked. My ears perked up, ready to note Jay's location.

Blade nodded. "Shall we join him?"

As we had planned, Katelyn was persistent. "Where on the ship?"

"Come with me and you'll see." Blade kept up the charm.

"I'm sorry. I'm nervous," Katelyn sighed. "I just want to know."

Scott squirmed next to me. "That loser isn't that big," he whispered.

Blade was losing patience. "Why? Why all the questions?"

Katelyn made a little girl face. "It's a big decision. Where is this Jay kid?"

Blade's anger burned through his facade and I caught a flash of his Jong face. Katelyn gripped the bleacher seat above us but kept her cool. Blade resumed his human image.

"In the toy room," he said and grabbed Katelyn's arm.

Katelyn yelled, "Hut one!"

Scott and I sprang out of the darkness, suited for battle in our pads and helmets. Scott hit Blade high while I dived low, knocking Blade off his feet. Katelyn sprinted out of reach.

Blade vaulted back up like a jack-in-the-box. Scott, hanging on the alien's back, was horrified as Blade transformed to his Jong self.

"He's a snake!" Scott cried. "A real snake!"

"You scared of snakes?" I said as I readied for a tackle.

Blade spun hard, hurling Scott off his back. "When they're seven feet tall I am!" Scott yelped as he bounced on the 50-yard line.

Blade and I circled each other. Barnabus crept from behind, armed with a lasso fashioned from the first-down marker chains. Without looking, Blade kicked back and flattened Barnabus.

Then he came for us, hissing and flicking. I pushed Katelyn behind me and took a three-point stance. Scott ran over and dropped down beside me.

"Come, Katelyn," Blade ordered.

"Schreiber. The duck play," I whispered.

Scott's face was dead blank. "Jeez. Duck?" He hadn't paid attention in practice.

"You divert, cut back. Hut one. Hut FOUR."

I dived for Blade's lower torso while Scott cut left. Blade turned to grab at him while I pushed and pushed. Blade twisted back, wrapped his arms around me, and squeezed. And squeezed some more.

"Come on, Schreiber," I gasped. Katelyn kicked at Blade's hands.

Scott charged from behind. Blade went down with a bang. "Quack that, snake," he gloated.

Blade staggered back up.

"Whoops. Quacked too soon," Scott yelped.

Blade closed in on the three of us, backing us

into the snack shed. Surrounded by trash cans on one side, the fence on the other, and the shed behind us, we had no escape. Blade reached for Katelyn.

"Take me instead," I begged.

"Too late, Pillsssssbury," Blade hissed. "I don't need you any more. But I still have room in my collection for a pretty little human girl."

I lunged at him but he tossed me back like a rag. He grabbed Katelyn's wrist and she screamed, a sound that tore my heart out. Then a shadow flitted from the haze.

Clink clink clink. The first-down chains fell over Blade's shoulder and slipped down around his arms. Barnabus stood behind the Jong, tugging. Scott and I got on the chain with him and within moments, the Jong was bound from his head to his countless toes with the first-down marker chains. After we secured him to the shack, we wrapped him in yards of medical tape.

"Let's go find Jay," I said.

Scott paused over Blade, who lay helpless in the grass. "You've just been sacked, ET."

Katelyn, Barnabus, and I trotted the perimeters of the ship's central chamber. Scott flattened against the wall.

Katelyn yelled, "I remember. This was the hall to the toy room!"

I jumped onto a light beam and dashed across.

Barnabus scurried from another angle. Scott remained stuck to the wall. "You gonna stay glued there all night, Schreiber?" I called.

"I'm coming," he said, his voice wavering. He stepped to the brink of the perimeter walkway but couldn't force his foot onto the light beam. I ran back across.

"Come on," I said. "I'll run interference." I ducked down as if I were about to block. Scott hesitated. "Come on, let's make that first down." I moved forward. Scott took a deep breath and came after me.

Moments later we were in the toy room. "Where is he?" Katelyn asked.

"Mike!" Jay was thirty feet above us, perched on a huge Frisbee. He started to cry. "That bad man put me up here."

"And I'm gonna get you down!" I promised. I lowered my voice. "But how the heck am I going to do it?" Katelyn shrugged and Barnabus looked blank.

Scott picked up a football-type toy. "Go out for a pass, Pillsbury."

"This isn't a game."

"Hey, the quarterback calls the plays," he said. "Go out for a pass!" He motioned toward the far wall. I ran across the floor, under Jay, toward the point Scott had indicated. Scott spiraled the ball up, toward Jay.

"Grab it, kid!" he yelled.

Jay leapt for the football. He wrapped his arms around it and held tight as the ball began its descent. Jay and the ball were spiraling toward me, too high. Way over my head. I bounded into the air and—

"And he scores!" Scott whooped.

Jay, the ball, and I tumbled to the ground, shaken but safe. Jay dropped the ball and wrapped his arms around me. "I'm scared."

"Don't worry," I said. "This story has a happy ending."

20

MINUTES LATER WE WERE AT THE SCRUNCHIE EXIT.
"Go ahead," I said to the group.

"What about you?" Katelyn asked.

"There's something I need to do."

"What you need to do, moron, is get out of here," Scott growled.

"Not yet," I said.

"Mike Pillsbury." Barnabus's tone was stern. "Once you leave the ship, I can grant you amnesty. Blade can't touch you. But while you're still inside . . ."

I was adamant. "There's something I have to do. You go ahead."

"I'm not leaving until I know you're safe," Barnabus said.

Katelyn folded her arms over her chest. "Me either."

I appealed to Scott's gallantry. "Schreiber. Help me. Take Katelyn and Jay out."

"Mike. Don't . . . " Katelyn pleaded. "Don't stay here."

"Please. Jay's had enough," I said. "He's got to get out. Please Katelyn. I know this seems weird to you but there's something I've got to do."

"Mike, whatever you need to do is all right with me." She took Jay from me, tears glistening in her eyes.

"Wait!" Barnabus ordered. He aimed his odd device at Katelyn. "On behalf of the Galactic Federation, I grant you amnesty." A white circle with a cross appeared on Katelyn's forehead.

He repeated the procedure with Scott and Jay. "Go quickly. Once you're out of the ship, Blade can't touch you."

"Run!" I yelped and they dashed for the exit.

Barnabus gave me a long look. "But as long as you are trespassing, Mike Pillsbury, you are fair game."

I laughed. "So call a Bom and sue me."

Weird or not, I had built my life around the Hanzel Chronicles. From the time I could daydream, I imagined ships from the sky, peaceful people longing for refuge, and villains oppressing the good folks of the galaxy. From the time I could talk, I told little stories about life on different planets and battles in outer space. As I grew older, the stories grew into the Chronicles and I developed a solid audience for the tales of the Hanzels, Jongs, and other folks from outer space.

I had wanted them to be true. I couldn't find my place on this Earth so I desperately hoped there would be a home for me out there, among the stars. But when I had my chance, I made a different choice: I stayed here.

And yet, the Jongs existed. We had seen one of them with our eyes and tasted their brand of evil. If the Jongs existed, what about the Hanzels?

I had to know.

Barnabus and I returned to the zoo room. Like a madman, I dashed from one display to the next. Barnabus, appalled by the number of caged species, growled and bared his teeth. "This is monstrous. I must report this to the Federation."

And then, I saw them. Looking very human with dark hair and eyes. Tall and slender, like me. Even in captivity their faces were peaceful and kind.

The Hanzels.

"I knew it! We've got to get them out," I shouted. "All of them!"

Barnabus searched for a release lever, some sort of lock or control. "I can't find the key," he moaned.

I threw myself against the panel. My brains rattled but the door didn't budge. Inside, the Hanzels turned as if they could sense something. "There must be a way," I said, frantic to find something to smash through the panel.

Suspended from the ceiling sixty feet up was a small room. A control room, I was sure. But I couldn't see any access to it. "Barnabus!"

He followed my pointing finger. Then he trotted out of the room.

"Fine time to disappear," I muttered as I continued to search for stairs or an elevator.

Nothing.

Barnabus returned, carrying a giant Frisbee.

"How convenient," said a voice behind him. We jerked toward the door, where Blade stood. "Right where I want you," he sneered.

"How did you get out of the chains?" I asked.

Blade smiled and unsheathed his fangs. A drop of fluid appeared, glistening like hot acid. I wasn't right about everything.

The Jongs *are* poisonous.

"The other humans may have been granted amnesty. But the Pillsbury is still available, I see." He slinked toward me, his many feet pattering softly while his upper body swayed with anticipation.

"Mike!" Barnabus barked. "Fetch!"

He spun the Frisbee into the air. As it rose, I jumped onto it. The Jong jerked backwards and slithered up the wall. I rode the Frisbee toward the control room. Closer and closer—but I wasn't close enough. I was going to miss it by about five feet.

I steadied myself, like a surfer riding a flying saucer. As I passed the tower I jumped and managed to grab a support beam. I hung by my hands, kicking and kicking, my legs flailing in the air. With a thrust worthy of a field goal kicker, I swung myself up and over.

The strut was about three inches wide. I tottered my way across and collapsed as I reached the control room. Blade slinked closer, coming straight across the ceiling. I forced myself up and ran to a panel that was covered with hundreds of buttons and alien gibberish.

I slapped the panel with both hands, pressing as many buttons as I could.

"Mike!" Barnabus shouted. Below me, the display panels slid open. Barnabus was in a frenzy, stamping each of the emerging captives with galactic amnesty.

I cheered. Then I gulped as Blade hissed in my ear.

"Sssssssurrender."

"Up yours," I said and punched the last button.

Blade unsheathed his laser sword. "I try to preserve specimens. But sometimes extermination is best."

He swung at my head. I dropped and rolled, sparks flying around me.

Blade took another swipe. I dived at the door and rolled out onto the strut. I hoisted myself up. Blade stood before me, the wall behind me, and the floor, now crowded with aliens, was a treacherous drop below me. It was surrender or die.

I had no intention of surrendering.

Blade raised his sword. "Here's how I grant amnesty," he hissed. The sword flashed down on me and I jumped off the strut.

I grabbed one of Blade's lower legs and swung in the air. He swept the sword toward me, barely missing me but burning through the strut. The strut buckled, then separated. I still held onto Blade's leg as he toppled. As he fell sideways, I let go and grabbed the strut.

Blade teetered, then regained his balance. I hung upside down, with my legs and arms wrapped around the strut. My narrow life preserver sank under my weight, threatening to dump me to the floor.

"We'll do this the old fashioned way," Blade said as he crept toward me. His tongue flicked and his fangs, dripping with venom, emerged. His hood rippled and his back hunched as he prepared to strike.

WHAP. Blade took a Frisbee in the face. He toppled from the strut and the aliens scattered as he fell hard to the floor.

Dead.

I glanced down and saw Barnabus smiling. The

strut wobbled and my legs let go. I began to slide off, about to follow Blade to his fate.

A Hanzel man called, *"Swebi. Swebi!"*

My fingers slipped, one by one.

All the Hanzels shouted in frantic chorus, *"Swebi!"*

In a flash of perfect clarity, I understood. But I couldn't obey. "I can't fly!" I cried as my last fingers ached to let go. "I'm not like you! I can't—"

My fingers let go.

"—fly!" I screamed.

And I flew.

21

Katelyn ran in, oblivious to the newly freed aliens. "Mike! Are you all right?"

"I'm fine," I said, only then understanding how entirely weird everything was. Weird but great.

Katelyn gasped as she realized she was in the middle of an alien horde. She gazed at the humanoids, lizards, bears, insects, stone lumps, leathery blobs, vegetable stalks. Some were twenty feet tall, some were the size of cats. There were orange spoon-headed llamas and purple-skinned spiders, blobs that smelled like Paris perfume and sleek eel-types that stunk like a sewer.

Barnabus nodded encouragement and they bowed at Katelyn.

"Um. Hello, everyone." She gave them her winning smile. "On behalf of Ashby Middle School, I bid you welcome." She dropped her voice and waved me and Barnabus closer. "We have a problem."

I groaned. "Not more aliens."

"Worse," she said. "People. Crowds of them out on the field. Here to see the UFO."

"What UFO?" I said, and then I knew. We were *in* the UFO.

Barnabus's translator box squealed. "We have to get these folks to my ship so I can arrange transport."

Katelyn sighed. "How are you going to move crowds of extraterrestrials through crowds of people? And still keep them a secret?"

Barnabus trotted in circles. I almost expected him to chase his own tail. "We can't risk a widespread sighting! If our presence becomes known, this planet will have to be . . ."

Katelyn and I gulped. Neutralized.

"Why can't you use this ship?" I asked.

"The Jongs booby trap everything. With Blade dead, this ship will self-destruct shortly," Barnabus answered. The ship rumbled. "Very shortly."

We were surrounded by amazing, bizarre, beautiful, and just plain weird creatures. Katelyn smiled at them but twisted her hands at us. "We can't parade them out for everyone to see."

What a sight. More extraterrestrials than even I had ever dreamed of. Than I had ever hoped for. Talk about a can of worms . . .

"Maybe we can," I said. "Maybe we can."

As Katelyn promised, the football field was packed with people, noisy, anxious, excited. A hush fell when I climbed from the ship. Mrs. Nickerson stepped out of the crowd. "Michael Pillsbury! What is the meaning of this?"

"Trust me," I said. "It's a surprise." I dodged through the mob and dashed into the field house. Scott and Jay were there.

"Pillsbury! You made it!" Scott whooped.

"Yeah," I said, slapping him on the back and hugging him. Then we remembered we were supposed to be enemies. We stared at each other, then laughed.

"Cool," Scott said. We slapped each other some more, then high-fived all around.

"What about the snake?" Scott asked.

"Dead."

"Good," Scott said.

"Good," Jay echoed.

I grabbed my laptop and double-clicked on the pumpkin icon. "Scott, can you help me out here?"

"Sure. What are friends for?"

As I ran back to Blade's ship, two policemen stepped in front of me. My eyes searched the milling people until I found Mrs. Nickerson. "Trust me," I called. She pulled the policemen back to let me pass.

Inside, the aliens were lined up and murmuring to get out. "Some of them have been captive a thousand years," Barnabus whispered. The ship's rumbling was now a steady roar.

"Get ready," I said. I stuck my head back outside and waved to Scott. He was across the field, at the controls in the field house. The scoreboard lit up with bright orange letters:

HAPPY HALLOWEEN, ASHBY

Then, the music started—"Ghoul's Night Out." Better late than never.

Listen to the werewolf howl
Beware, you'll see the monster scowl
The vampire grins a toothy smile
The zombie spins in deadpan style

Watch out! They're out!
They're coming out to play.
So don't get in their way
It's Ghoul's night out.

The crowd went dead silent. And then the people filled the cool night with rousing cheers.

The classic Frankensteins, Draculas, and Werewolves danced on the scoreboard. I nodded at Katelyn and she stepped out of the ship. Like a homecoming queen, she waved to the people. Then she motioned behind her.

Out came the parade of aliens.

The people *oohed* and *aahed* and gasped.

Mrs. Nickerson nudged me. "The costumes look so real!"

"Don't they?" I said, trying to keep a straight face.

The paraders marched across the field. Katelyn waved high and low and the aliens followed suit, some waving tentacles, others waving claws, still others flapping wings.

The football field rocked with "Ghoul's Night Out."

An exuberant Hanzel floated into the air. I jumped up and pulled him back down. "Trumpwot," he said.

"You're welcome," I replied.

As the parade marched through the gate and into the parking lot, Scott and Jay came out of the field house, decked out in football gear. They joined the end of the parade.

At the far end of the field there was a burst of flame. Blade's ship self-destructed, disappearing into a sprinkle of sparks. "Fireworks!" Mrs. Nickerson exclaimed.

The only onlooker who wasn't enjoying the show was Nick Thorpe. His arms were crossed and his face was sour. I couldn't blame him—there I was with Scott and Katelyn, leaving him out.

"Nick, come here," I yelled.

Barnabus nudged my leg. "Mike. You can't—"

"He's one of us," I said. "He knew about you a long time ago."

Nick strolled over casually as if he didn't care to be there. "Nice of you to get around to inviting me to hang out."

I pulled him into line behind one of our newly freed captives. Nick tripped over a tentacle that trailed from a "cheerleader's" skirt. "Hey, watch out," Nick yelled. Then he stopped cold when the eye on the end of the tentacle winked at him. Nick grabbed me. "The stories," he panted.

I smiled and shrugged. "Here they are. It's got to be our secret. No one else can know."

Nick's eyes were wide with awe. He ran up and down the parade, peeking into helmets and pushing aside pom-poms. Then he came back to me. "I'm sorry," he said. "I thought you were making them up."

"So did I," I laughed.

"Well, nice job," he said and headed back to the crowd of onlookers.

"Wait!" I yelled. "We could use some help, keeping the parade going."

"Hey, what are friends for?" Nick grinned.

What are friends for? I could tell a whole chronicle on that subject.

We marched on, past the school and then on to the streets of town. Kids ran out of their houses, tugging costumes over their pajamas. Adults grabbed masks or tied bandannas on their faces. Some folks carried pumpkins. The parade grew longer and longer. Boom boxes appeared to replace the music we had left behind at the field.

At the corner of West and Dow streets, Mom, Dad, and Jill came screeching to a stop in Dad's BMW.

"Mike! We were worried sick," Dad said. Mom wrapped her arms around me and squeezed hard.

"Not to worry," I said. "We were just working on the parade."

Even Jill smiled as the aliens passed by, in their bright colors and bizarre faces. "This is so unbelievable," she said. "Super."

"You organized this event, Mike?" Mom asked.

"Yep."

"Amazing," she said.

"Outstanding," Dad said as he squeezed me, too. "You did such a good job, you could almost believe it was all real."

"Mom and Dad. Try. Try to believe," I said.

My parents looked at each other and smiled. "We'll try," Mom said.

Jill pulled a lipstick from her pocket and drew hearts on her cheeks.

"What're you doing?" I asked.

"Joining the parade," she said with a smile. "It's awesome, Mike." She jumped in and rocked with her friends. Dad locked the car while Mom fashioned broad-brimmed sailor hats out of the *Wall Street Journal*. They swept along with the celebrating crowds, waving to me as they went.

It was a joyous midnight surprise for Ashby.

Our first annual Halloween parade.

22

At the town center, Katelyn and I diverted the aliens out of the parade and down a side street. Barnabus waited for us at the used car lot. Next to his ship was an elaborate star gate. The aliens rushed to it and stepped through, one by one.

"Where did you get that?" I asked.

"The Boms donated it," Barnabus replied.

"That was nice of them," Katelyn remarked.

Barnabus snorted. "Don't be deceived. The Boms are on the other side of the gate, lining the released captives up for a whopper of a class action suit against the Jongs."

The extraterrestrials disappeared too quickly. I was happy they were free but sorry to see them go. That old regret hammered at my chest. Would I ever see such sights again in my life?

The Hanzels were last in line. Their leader, a man named Bartle, nodded to me. *"Sharnin?"*

"What?" I asked.

Barnabus translated. "He wants to know if you're going with them."

I could feel the tug of kinship. "I don't know. Where do I belong?"

"You tell me," Barnabus said.

I saw it so clearly—the planet of peace to which the Hanzels would finally return. The people who could fly and breathe underwater. The most honest merchants in the galaxy.

But I could also see Jay waiting for a story and Nick clowning around. Scott, a new friend who shared this weird night with us. I closed my eyes and thought of my parents, who wanted everything good for me. My sister, Jill, and the music in her voice as she danced in the parade. And Katelyn, who truly understood my heart.

"Here. This is where I belong," I said.

Barnabus nodded. "A very intelligent decision." He spoke to Bartle. *"Luka none."*

Bartle hugged me good-bye. *"Yuhja muni."*

"Long life to you, too," I said. He was through the gate before I realized—

"Barnabus! Why did I understand him? And how did I fly?"

Barnabus just smiled that dog star smile. And

I knew what I had always known—that the universe is filled with mysteries and miracles.

The lights on the star gate flickered, then died. It disappeared into itself and was gone. Barnabus stepped onto the ramp to his ship.

"You're leaving, too?" Katelyn asked.

Barnabus nodded. "This planet has resumed protected status. I've got to vacate the premises."

"Will we ever see you again?" Scott asked.

"Perhaps, if your planet ever becomes worthy of galactic citizenship. There's a wonderful universe out there, just waiting for people like you."

I bent over to hug Barnabus, then remembered. I stepped back. "Sorry. No casual contact."

"I can make an exception," Barnabus said.

Katelyn and I hugged him tight. Jay petted him and Scott shook his paw.

Barnabus stepped inside his ship. "Work hard at helping your planet to grow up. I don't want to have to wait light years to see you all again."

He closed the door.

We backed away and watched as the spaceship sputtered up and away. We followed its light until it disappeared into the stars.

23

THe NeXt aFterNooN was Warm aNd PeaCeFuL. IN a couple of hours, kids would be donning masks and costumes and heading out for trick-or-treat. Katelyn and I would pass out candy at my house. But first, we shared a quiet moment in the treehouse.

We had two straws and one can of soda. That was okay, because Katelyn and I liked the same kind of soda, the same kind of cookies. We liked different movies, the same books, different sports— well, it didn't matter, because we were friends.

"What's up?" Nick said as he plopped over the ladder. Katelyn and I bumped heads. Nick noticed Katelyn and said, "Oh. I'll lose myself."

"Wait!" I called.

"Plenty of room," Katelyn said.

The squirts popped up behind him. "Katelyn, meet Danny, Ben, and Kurt," I said.

Katelyn winked. "And my friend Jay."

Jay winked back. We made room for everyone.

"So when am I going to hear one of your stories, Mike?" Katelyn asked.

Ben's face turned dark. "Can she be trusted?"

Nick snickered. "How do we know she won't turn you in to the Jongs?"

Katelyn, Jay, and I laughed so hard the tree shook. Nick smacked me with the foam football. "Come on, dude, get on with the story."

I leaned back.

Did I ever tell you about the time—

"Hey! Anyone up there?" We all looked over the side. Scott stood at the bottom of the ladder. I glanced at Nick.

"Him, too?" Nick asked.

"Okay with you?" I asked.

"What the heck? Why not?" he said. "Like Katelyn said, any friend."

"Beam yourself up, Scottie," I yelled. We made room for everyone, tight but happy. And then I began.

It was on a planet very much like Earth where the Jongs finally met their match. . . .

They're super-smart, they're super-cool, and they're *aliens*!
Their job on our planet? To try and rescue the...

RU1:2
79729-1/$3.99 US/$4.99 Can

THE HUNT IS ON
79730-5/$3.99 US/$4.99 Can

ALL HANDS ON DECK
79732-1/$3.99 US/$4.99 Can

SPITTING IMAGE
79733-X/$3.99 US/$4.99 Can

RABID TRANSIT
79734-8/$3.99 US/$4.99 Can

UNDER LOCH AND KEY
79735-6/$3.99 US/$4.99 Can

SPELL BOUND
79736-4/$3.99 US/$4.99 Can

SPACE RACE
79737-2/$3.99 US/$5.50 Can

DOUBLE TROUBLE
80725-4/$3.99 US/$5.50 Can

DISORDERLY CONDUCT
80726-2/$3.99 US/$5.50 Can

JOIN IN THE ADVENTURES WITH BUNNICULA AND HIS PALS
by James Howe

HOWLIDAY INN

69294-5/ $4.99 US/ $6.99 Can

THE CELERY STALKS AT MIDNIGHT

69054-3/ $4.99 US/ $7.50 Can

RETURN TO HOWLIDAY INN

71972-X/ $4.99 US/ $6.99 Can

DON'T MISS ANY OF THE STORIES BY AWARD-WINNING AUTHOR AVI

Join in the Wild and Crazy Adventures with Some Trouble-Making Plants

by Nancy McArthur

THE PLANT THAT ATE DIRTY SOCKS
75493-2/ $4.50 US/ $6.50 Can

**THE RETURN OF THE PLANT
THAT ATE DIRTY SOCKS**
75873-3/ $3.99 US/ $4.99 Can

**THE ESCAPE OF THE PLANT
THAT ATE DIRTY SOCKS**
76756-2/ $3.99 US/ $4.99 Can

**MORE ADVENTURES OF THE PLANT
THAT ATE DIRTY SOCKS**
77663-4/ $3.99 US/ $4.99 Can

**THE PLANT THAT ATE DIRTY SOCKS
GOES UP IN SPACE**
77664-2/ $4.50 US/ $6.50 Can

**THE MYSTERY OF THE PLANT
THAT ATE DIRTY SOCKS**
78318-5/ $3.99 US/ $4.99 Can

**THE PLANT THAT ATE DIRTY SOCKS
GETS A GIRLFRIEND**
78319-3/ $3.99 US/ $4.99 Can

**THE PLANT THAT ATE DIRTY SOCKS
GOES HOLLYWOOD**
79935-9/ $3.99 US/ $5.50 Can